IGNITING THEIR HEARTS

MEN OF BLACKTHORNE MOUNTAIN BOOK 2

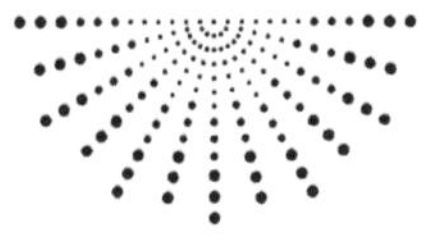

CAMERON HART

❀ Created with Vellum

*

They'd walk through fire to save the woman who ignited their hearts.

Austin: I may have rescued Tasha from a fire, but I'm no hero. My best friend, Flynn, and I have been firefighters for years. We've saved dozens of people, but no one quite like her.

I'm not sure why I sat by Tasha in the hospital until she woke up or why she gazed at me with something close to awe. If she knew my whole sordid tale, she'd never look at me the same way again.

Flynn thinks Tasha is perfect for us, but I gave up hope of finding love years ago. I don't deserve it, and certainly not from someone as pure as Tasha.

Flynn: She's soft, sweet, innocent perfection. Tasha. My queen. Austin pulled her from the fire and placed her in my arms, exactly where she belongs.

Our girl is still recovering from the mysterious fire that broke out in her office. Things aren't adding up, and we'll get to the bottom of it. Austin and I will keep Tasha safe, no matter what. Then we'll keep her, period.

Tasha: I woke up to not one, but two hulking firefighter mountain men by my hospital bed. At first, I thought I must have been dreaming, but then the pain of my injuries sank in.

Flynn always has a grin on his handsome face as well as a joke to make me laugh. His sparkling blue eyes pull me in, drag me under, and drown me in their warmth. And then there's Austin. His dark eyes follow me wherever I go, watching, studying, protecting.

The longer I'm around these men, the deeper I fall under their spell. I can't choose between them, and they tell me I don't have to. Can our fragile relationship survive threats both old and new?

WANT A FREE BOOK?

Sign up for my newsletter and get your copy of Chasing Stacy.

River: One look at the stunning waitress carrying the weight of the world on her shoulders, and I'm a gonner. I wasn't looking for a sweet little thing with auburn hair and more baggage than I can fit on the back of my bike, but there's no going back now. She's mine. I'll prove to her I'm more than capable of handling her past and making her feel safe again.

CONNECT WITH ME!

Check out my website, cameronhart.net, for sneak previews on my latest projects.

Follow me on social media:

Facebook Page
Facebook Group
Instagram
Goodreads
Bookbub

Sign up for my street team to receive ARCs & help spread the word about new releases.

Edited by: CM Wheary Editing
Website: https://cmwheary.com/
Instagram: @cmwhearyediting

CHAPTER 1

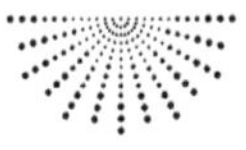

TASHA

I take a swig of coffee, sputtering and choking it down when I realize it's gone cold. I swear I just made it five minutes ago, but one look at the clock in the corner of my computer screen lets me know it's been over two hours. I often get lost in my thoughts, but today of all days?

Sighing, I look down at the now ruined beverage and frown. It took all of my courage to stop by the breakroom this morning and make myself coffee in the first place. I even got into the office an extra fifteen minutes early to make sure I was the only one here.

It's not that I don't like people; I'm just so self-conscious and cripplingly shy around others that I can't seem to take a breath without overthinking every little detail. Starting conversations with strangers is an actual recurring nightmare I have. I shiver just thinking about it. *What is appropriate small talk? What do I do with my hands? Can they tell I'm sweating? Has my laugh always been that shrill?*

And the nightmare isn't over once the conversation stops. Oh, no. On the rare occasion I interact with other humans, every embarrassing word plays in a loop in my head as I try to go to sleep at night for weeks afterward. It's in everyone's best interest for me to go about unnoticed, and honestly, I've become quite good at it.

Growing up in foster care taught me a lot about blending in. Not all of my foster families were terrible, but none of them were particularly welcoming. I learned early on to follow the rules and not make things more difficult for anyone.

I aged out of the system two and a half years ago and managed to land a scholarship to USD Community College for business accounting. Numbers are my happy place. They never change. The rules are concrete and knowable. I never have to worry about making a fool of myself as long as I know which numbers I can plug into an equation.

People, on the other hand, are much more complicated and unpredictable. I've had enough instability in my life, so I'll stick to my numbers, *thankyouverymuch*.

I give my nasty coffee one last long look before setting it aside. I'll just try again tomorrow. There's no way I'd step foot inside the breakroom now. It's nearly eleven in the morning—prime coffee refill time for the other accountants on the third floor. A shiver runs down my spine at the thought of walking into the kitchen and seeing Katie and Sarah gossiping about anything and everything. Most likely me.

And God forbid I bump into my new boss, Harry. A cold sweat breaks out on my brow at the reminder of our last meeting. I've only been working at the Blackthorne Lumber Distribution Center for a few months, but I'm already on thin ice with my boss.

I landed a job in their accounting department as soon as I graduated with my associate degree. I made the mistake of double-checking the work of the last person in my job. Like I said, I'm good with numbers and patterns, so I easily spotted some lines in our last audit that didn't add up. After further investigation, it appeared that the guy previously in my position, Nate, was skimming off the top.

Of course, I triple and even quadruple-checked my findings before saying anything. I'm not normally one to speak up, but this was some serious theft that had gone on for quite some time. Plus, I didn't want anyone to look over the number trail years down the road and associate my name with this shady bookkeeping.

In any case, I thought I was doing the right thing by telling Harry about the discrepancies in numbers. Instead of thanking me for bringing it up, Harry said I needed to stick in my lane and only do the tasks assigned to me. He seemed offended, though that wasn't my intention at all. If one of my former employees had done shoddy work, I'd want to know. But for some reason, Harry became visibly agitated.

I close my eyes and take a deep, cleansing breath, trying to block out the memory. His face had turned a mottled red, the tendons in his neck bulging as he spat at me to keep my head down and not make waves.

Stupid me. I *never* make waves, and the first time I tried speaking up about something I thought was important, I got shut down. Figures. I was beyond mortified after that meeting with my boss and have kept to myself, quietly working away in my cubicle ever since. I come into the office a few minutes before anyone, eat lunch alone at my desk, and leave after the others have filed out.

Lonely and a bit pathetic, yes, but comfortable. Familiar. A routine I can settle into. That's about as much as someone like me can hope to get out of life. I have too many quirks and insecurities to make friends, let alone be in a relationship. God, I'm flushed with embarrassment just thinking about flirting, or heaven forbid, *kissing* someone. I'm sure I'd be terrible at it. How does one kiss and breathe at the same time? Do you both gasp for air together? Or breathe in each other's breath?

Ugh. See? I'm far too awkward and stuck in my head to be any good at relationship stuff. I've mostly accepted it, though. I don't need a man to be content. I just need myself, my numbers, and a good book to settle down with at the end of a long day.

"Aren't you coming?"

I gasp and jump out of my seat, twisting in the direction of the voice in the doorway. Katie glares at me and lifts a perfectly manicured eyebrow as she eyes me up and down. She's beautiful in her tight black pencil skirt and pink satin blouse. Her blonde hair is perfectly curled and styled, swept to the side in a romantic look.

I know what she sees when she looks at me. Clearance rack dress pants that are a size too small and a blazer that has seen better days. It's hard finding plus-size professional clothes and even harder finding them on sale or at thrift shops. Compared to her, I look like a fat, frumpy mess.

"Uh...where?" I squeak out, unsure of what she's talking about. My cheeks grow hot and sweat dampens the back of my neck. *Go away, go away, go away,* my anxious brain repeats, wishing I could hide under my desk. Like I said, I'm not good around people for any amount of time.

"The all-company brunch. We go out every quarter on the boss's dime."

"I didn't get an email about it," I murmur, turning back to my computer and scrolling through my inbox. Nope, no email, no invite, nothing. Part of me is hurt that no one thought to invite me out to brunch, but the bigger part of me is relieved. Going out with my coworkers sounds like a recipe for disaster, especially if food is involved. I'm already so self-conscious of my extra weight, there's no way I'd be able to eat anything in front of anyone.

"Oh. Hmm." Katie already sounds bored. Sure enough, when I look up at her, she's picking her nails and getting ready to leave. "You can still come if you want. Or not. Whatever."

I'm about to respectfully decline her invitation, but she's already walking away before she even finishes her sentence.

When I hear the elevator doors close with a ding, I slump back in my chair. I hardly spoke ten words and yet my heart is racing as if I just ran up a flight of stairs. My back is drenched in cold sweat and my hands are shaking slightly.

Deep breath in, two, three, four. Hold it, two, three, four. Let it out, two, three, four.

I repeat the breathing exercise a few more times until I'm not so light-headed. Maybe I'll take advantage of the guaranteed empty break room to see if we have tea options. I probably shouldn't drink any more coffee. I'm jittery enough as it is.

With one last cleansing breath, I force myself up from my chair, wincing slightly at my tense muscles. Good Lord, all Katie had to do was mention hanging out with my coworkers and I all but spiraled out of control.

I make my way toward the bathroom on shaky legs, resting my palms on the counter once I get inside. I try not to look at myself in the mirror as I take a few more breaths, and then splash some cold water on my face and neck. I've never been a pretty girl, and that's okay. But I don't want to see what Katie just saw. I don't want to look at myself through her eyes any more than I already do.

I can't seem to help it, though. Wide green eyes stare back at me from the mirror, glassy with unshed tears. My cheeks and neck are bright red and itchy, a fun side effect of my extreme social anxiety. The look is complete with my flat, strawberry blonde hair sticking to the sides of my damp face.

I look like a frightened, drowned mouse. I feel like one most days, too.

After patting down my face and washing my hands, I'm pleased to discover a stash of chamomile tea in the breakroom. I take my time getting it exactly how I like it, knowing I'll probably never have the breakroom all to myself in the middle of the day again. If everyone else is out having fun, I can, too—right?

I scoff at myself and my idea of *fun.* Making chamomile tea and scrolling through my phone alone in the breakroom. I'm living the introvert's dream, let me tell you.

Something pulls me from the rabbit hole I dug myself into while scrolling. Or, rather, the naked mole rat hole I dug myself into. I'm not even sure why I started reading this article in the first place, but these little guys are amazing. They have teeth on the outside of their lips so they can dig without eating dirt. How crazy is that?

But then I hear that crackling sound again, and this time it's followed by an odd smell. Burning plastic? Oh my God, is that *smoke* in the hallway?!

I leap out of my chair, discarding my phone and empty tea mug, and charge into the hallway.

"Oh no," I gasp softly as I make my way into the main room with our cubicles.

I'm frozen in place, tears stinging my eyes as I watch smoke billow from the storage room in back. I can see orange light glowing from somewhere deep inside, and then a few flames lick the doorframe, leaping onto a stack of papers on the file cabinet along the back wall.

"No, no, no," I repeat, my hands covering my mouth in shock. What did I do to cause this? It has to be my fault, right? I'm the only one on this floor and have been for the last hour.

A hollow laugh escapes me before I choke back a sob. *Oh God, I'm going to get fired. Because of a FIRE!*

I'm not sure what I'm doing, but my body moves forward without my permission, carrying me toward the clusterfuck of a situation. Why aren't there any fire alarms going off? Shouldn't we have a sprinkler system or something in place? Dammit, what do I do?

In the time it takes me to run to the door of the storage room, the flames have completely taken over. Heat emanates from within the cavern of flames and smoke, making me stumble backward and trip on my worn-out heels.

I go down hard, hitting the ground with a thud that knocks the wind out of me. Scrambling backward, I gasp for air and choke on thick, black smoke. Crawling on my hands and knees to the first cubicle I can find, I pick up the desk phone and dial 911. The phone slips out of my sweaty hand, but I grab it back up and focus on my breathing.

"911, please state your name, address, and emergency," comes the calm female voice on the other end of the line.

"T-Ta-sh-sha," I stutter out, each breath stinging my lungs as I pull smoke down with the oxygen. "Tasha Baxter."

"Tasha, what—"

"Fire!" I cough, the heat of the flames at my back making me feel claustrophobic. "Fire at Blackthorne Lumber Distribution Center. It's...it's located..." I pause, out of breath, sweat pouring down my face and dripping into my mouth.

"Thirteen-forty-two Pine Street," the woman fills in for me. I nod, then remember she can't see me.

"Yes," I whisper, my voice scratchy. "I-I think I need to leave."

"Are you inside?" she asks, more than a little alarmed.

"Yes," I choke out. "Third floor. I'm—"

An ominous crack tears through the dense atmosphere and I look directly up just in time to see part of the ceiling cave in. I shriek and roll out of the way as plaster, wood, and fiberglass crash down around me.

I'm gripping the phone tightly, though I ripped it off its cord when I rolled over, effectively cutting off my only source of communication with the outside world. Everything in me wants to give up, to curl up in a ball and let the flames engulf me, body and soul. Life has been nothing but a string of disappointments and painful lessons. Maybe this is how it's supposed to end. Maybe I'm not meant to keep fighting so hard just to exist.

I lay there, listening to flames eat away thousands of dollars' worth of computers and equipment, not to mention *years* of paper records we were only just beginning to transfer into digital copies.

Get. Up.

My heart jumps to life, pounding those two words into my ribcage over and over. *Get up. Get up. Get up.*

I groan, every muscle protesting the thought of moving, let alone continuing to scrape by in my pathetic life.

Get up. Get up. Get up.

No, I can't. What am I even fighting for anymore? Another day at a job where no one remembers to invite me out to brunch, even though I'm too anxious to hang out anyway? Another week living in my shitty apartment I can barely afford? Another month living paycheck to paycheck trying to squeak by any way that I can? Another year in a miserable, inconsequential life?

Get up. Get up. Get up.

My arms reach out, fingers digging into the carpet as I pull myself up onto my hands and knees. I don't want to keep going. I want to disappear inside the smoke. No more anxiety. No more pain. No more doubting every single thought, word, and action.

My body won't give up, however. Though my brain

protests every movement, I find myself crawling through the debris, keeping low to the ground as I navigate my way toward the door to the stairs.

Keep going. Keep going. Keep going.

"No," I stubbornly grit out, the single word sending me into a coughing fit. I double over, clawing at my neck as I inhale sharply. Each breath burns my lungs, and still, I trudge forward. As much as I want to sink back onto the floor and let death claim me, there's something else at work here. Some long dormant part of me that decided to show up, take charge, and fight to the bitter end.

Keep going. Keep going. Keep going.

I can see the edge of the stairway now, though my vision is dimming by the second. I can't tell if it's the smoke making everything darker or if I'm about to pass out. Either way, I'm so close. So damn close.

Almost there...

A sickening snap cracks through the room a second before a rush of air surrounds me, followed by a thundering crash. All of my senses are on overload, and it takes me a moment to realize what happened.

A support beam fell right in front of me, the flames jumping up five feet in the air, blocking my exit. I open my mouth to scream, but all that comes out is a scratchy, guttural groan that scrapes my throat on the way out.

Trapped. I'm trapped. When it was my choice to give up, I felt a bit of peace. Now that I'm stuck here, my claustrophobia kicks up a notch. My mind flashes to my first foster family, where I slept in a closet. They locked me in there at night and I always worried they'd forget about me come morning.

My clothes feel itchy and too tight, like they are cutting off my air supply. My fingers twitch and my skin crawls as I resist the urge to tear everything off in an attempt to break free from my mental and physical prison.

I'm losing my damn mind; thoughts, fears, and panic are swimming in my head and veins. My breaths are choppy and uneven, each one more painful than the last. My lungs feel shredded, like I swallowed a bunch of broken glass. Each time I swallow feels like pouring salt into an open wound.

A siren pierces through my blurry thoughts, but I think it's too late to save me. Hopefully, everyone else got out in time. I have no idea how the fire started, but if I go down with it, it'll be a clean-cut case, right? My fault, and I paid for my transgressions. At least I'll have died like I lived—pathetically making things easy for everyone else around me.

Footsteps thunder up the stairs as men shout over each other. I'm barely aware of the chaos surrounding me, my eyes nearly glued shut from my drying tears. Dragging shallow, painful breaths through my lungs, I try inching forward again before collapsing on the ground.

Thud. Thud. Thud.

I'm not sure if it's the sound of my fading heartbeat or of boots stomping up the stairs, but I don't have any strength left to keep my eyes open. My body feels heavy with resignation. This is it. No more fighting. No more floundering. Just...nothingness.

"I've got you," a deep voice surrounds me, wrapping around my body and soul and squeezing me back to life. I whimper when I feel myself being lifted, my heavy limbs curling around something solid. "Don't talk," the voice says, firm and commanding. "I've got you," he repeats, putting an end to my rioting thoughts.

I manage to pry one eye open, my vision blurry at best. Still, I see dark brown eyes lock on mine—intense, focused, and in control. I can't process anything else about the man currently cradling me to his chest, but those eyes will forever be branded in my memory, singeing my very soul and setting it on fire.

Such depth and determination, an almost primal need to get me to safety. He stares at me for a split second longer before I feel his hand come behind my head, urging me to press my face against his shoulder.

"I'll keep you safe, little one," he murmurs. His words are a bit mumbled from the mask he's wearing, but I hear them all the way down in my heart. I have no reason to believe him, but I do. This man will keep me safe. Me. His little one.

It's the last thought I have before I fall into the black abyss.

CHAPTER 2

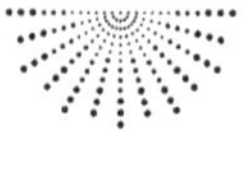

FLYNN

"Goddamnit, Austin," I mutter to myself as I sprint after my best friend. I've been following him into burning buildings for over eight years now, and it's always the same.

Austin goes for the most dangerous parts of the mission. If there's a chance of a collapsing roof, he'll be the one to hold it up until everyone gets to safety. If a car flipped over on the highway and burst into flames, Austin will be there, prying the doors open with his bare hands.

To say he has a hero complex is the understatement of the century, though he'd never admit it. The man hates being called a hero, for starters.

No number of lives saved will make up for the one he lost all those years ago. He was just fourteen, and there's nothing else he could have done to save his sister. But nearly two decades later, Austin is still seeking redemption.

I quickly scan the reception area on the first floor of the Blackthorne Lumber Distribution Center, noting that it's empty and there doesn't seem to be any smoke or fire damage. We were told the call came from someone on the third floor of the four-story building. Thankfully, the fire seems to be isolated. With the lumber mill not far from the distribution center, this could have been the worst fire this small mountain town has ever seen.

As it is, the poor woman who reported the fire was inside when she made the call, which got disconnected about twenty seconds in. I know Austin's only goal is to get to the woman before the fire claims another life.

The door to the stairwell slams shut, grabbing my attention. Two other guys in our unit spread out, searching the first floor for anyone hiding while I continue toward the stairs. Austin shouldn't be going up there alone, and he fucking knows it. I swear the man is going to make me go gray before I turn thirty-five next year.

He doesn't have a death wish as much as a complete disregard for his own life. Austin is a man of few words, but his eyes say it all. He feels to his very core he was supposed to die instead of his sister, so he doesn't see the problem with throwing himself into any and every dangerous situation if it means saving someone else.

It's noble, sure, and yes, he's saved dozens of people. But he's reckless. Careless with the life he's been given. The man is so concerned with saving everyone around him, he doesn't see he's the one in danger half the goddamn time.

Austin is my best friend, closer than a brother to me. He needs me to watch over him, and not just when he's leaping up stairs three at a time and hurdling headlong into the flames like he is now. I hold my breath and quicken my pace as I watch the broken but determined bastard enter the third floor, which is about to explode from the fire raging inside.

I'm five steps from the top of the stairs when Austin emerges through the doorway carrying a fucking angel.

She's cradled against his chest with her head tucked into his shoulder to protect her face. I can only make out her silhouette through the smoke and flickering flames, but there's something about her that feels...life-giving. Like that first breath of clean oxygen after fighting a fire.

"Take her," Austin shouts, startling the woman. He closes the distance between us and tries transferring her to my arms, but she coughs and clings to him, burying her face into the side of his neck.

My heart twists up painfully for the woman. I can feel her fear and confusion as much as the scorching fire surrounding us. Unfortunately, there isn't time to comfort her with kind words and reassurances.

I reach out for her, prying her arms from around Austin's neck. To my absolute shock, Austin looks like he's hurting as much as she is when I finally gather her into my embrace. That's new.

"You're in good hands," Austin says to the woman, straining to be heard through his mask and the growing inferno around us. "You're safe," he promises.

I'm too stunned to move at first. He's providing words of comfort? I didn't know he was even aware of other people's feelings, let alone had the capacity to soothe someone. Austin grips my shoulder, shaking me slightly and snapping me back into the moment. His deep brown eyes bore into me, and I somehow know what he's thinking. *Her safety is the most important thing. Don't fuck it up.*

With a determined nod, I turn and stride downstairs, my only mission in life to get this woman outside and away from danger. She whimpers and coughs, violent shivers wracking her body as I press it against my own.

Jesus Christ. Her tortured cries rip me apart, tearing up my insides until I'm one big bleeding heart for her. I never want to let her go. The mere thought of never seeing her again has me swallowing back panic.

In all my thirty-four years, I've never had this reaction to someone before. I know for damn sure Austin's never acted this way, either, like he wants to be gentle with her. I have no idea what it means, but my head fills with possibilities as I break through the front door of the building and into the parking lot.

In the afternoon light, I can see more of the woman's features. I study her as I make my way to the ambulance on standby. Her face is covered in ash and tinged in pink, but there's no mistaking her delicate features.

A small, cute little button nose dots her face, along with perfect cupid's bow lips. Her brow furrows as she tries opening her eyes. I set her down on the waiting stretcher, though it takes the rest of my diminishing strength to loosen my hold on her.

Taking off my mask, I look down at the shivering woman, noticing for the first time her blazer is half torn off and she has no shoes on.

"I'm going to put this oxygen mask on you now, miss," the EMT, Brent, says.

The angel's eyes snap open—wide, green, and laced with panic. She's undeniably gorgeous and utterly terrified. I step forward, hoping to comfort her, but she flinches away from me. Holy fuck, that hurts, but I understand. This is one of the worst days of her life. She nearly died. We still don't know the extent of her injuries. I remind myself of all of this, though I still have to rub the heel of my hand over my heart to ease the tightness there from her rejection.

"You're safe now," I manage to croak out, drawing her attention toward me. She trembles and then starts shaking her head frantically, tears streaming down her face. Her eyes dart around the parking lot, like she's searching for someone. "You were the last one in the building," I say, hoping to ease her worry. "Austin is doing the final check, but you were the only one hurt."

The woman doesn't say anything, she just keeps looking

around her and sucking down ragged breaths. She's going to pass out if we don't get the oxygen mask on her, but she can't seem to sit still.

"The mask will help you breathe easier while we assess the damage," Brent tries again, holding the mask up to her face. She winces and I growl, grabbing it from him. I don't like her being afraid of anyone, and while the scared little angel doesn't seem to trust me, the least I can do is make sure no one else intimidates her.

"You're a fighter," I tell her, looking into her wide, emerald eyes. "You survived a fire," I continue when she holds eye contact with me. "That's pretty badass." She blinks a few times but remains still. I hold the mask out again, and this time she lets me secure it around her as she takes a few shallow breaths. The woman chokes on a cough and I'm right there, rubbing her back and trying to soothe her any way I can.

She turns on her side, whimpering and kicking out her legs. I can tell she's so damn exhausted that she's nearly delusional. Brent looks like he's about to touch my girl. I grunt at him to give her some space. He gives me a weird look but backs off.

I'm about to reach out and try to comfort her again, but she freezes, the breath caught in her throat. I think she might have passed out again, but then I look up and see Austin storming through the crowd of firefighters and first responders, his nearly black eyes narrowing in on the ambulance.

I watch in complete fascination as he strides toward the woman lying on the stretcher in front of me. I swear I can feel their connection almost as much as I feel my own connection to her. The sight of him eases some of the tension in the little angel's curvy body. I can feel her anxiety fade ever so much, though I have no fucking clue how I know that.

I don't have any room to be jealous when Austin is standing next to us, looking down at the woman he pulled from the flames with equal parts desire and worry. His hand hovers over her, like he wants to touch her but isn't sure he's allowed to.

She stares up at him, her green eyes pleading for...*something.* I don't think she even knows what she needs, but Austin and I will do anything for her. The obsession is setting in. I feel it and don't even try fighting it. I don't want to. All I want is to be a part of whatever fragile hope we all found in the midst of the flames.

Austin has been growing more and more distant with each passing year, burrowing deeper into the darkness and grief that have never left his heart. I convinced him to move out here to Blackthorne Mountain with me about five years ago in an attempt to shake him up a bit and get him out of the depression that had clouded his mind.

We bought a cabin halfway up the mountain, close enough to town to make it into our shifts at the fire station without much of a commute. I heard about the little mountain town in South Dakota from my mother, who had followed Clayton Stanford all the way out here for a job.

I grew up on the Stanford estate with my mom, who worked as their housekeeper, though I haven't seen much of Clayton since his ex fucked him over a decade ago. He left town and built a fortress up on Blackthorne Mountain to hide out. My mother, ever the meddling woman, stormed up there with him and refused to leave.

These days, Ma only works part-time as Clayton's housekeeper. He's got a woman up there with him now, Naomi. Sweet girl, and totally in love with Clayton's grumpy ass. Though he's not nearly as growly as he used to be. In fact, my mom says he even smiles and tells the occasional joke.

What I wouldn't give to have a woman love me so much

she seeps into the foundation of who I am and changes me for the better. Austin, too. I didn't think we'd ever have that. Austin is...unstable sometimes. He needs me to temper him and pull him back from that dangerous place in his mind. How would a woman fit into that dynamic?

Looking back down at the woman lying between us, something settles in place. She's what we've been missing. I don't know how or why or what that even means, but my life is inexplicably tied to hers now, just like it's been tied to Austin's since we were kids.

Austin's hand shakes slightly as he brushes some of her strawberry blonde hair out of her face, revealing more of her beauty to us. I've never seen him be this tender with anyone. She seems to sense the gravity of what's happening, even in her panicked state. Her hand covers his and she nuzzles into his palm, closing her eyes and finally taking a full breath.

Austin looks at me, the shock in his eyes almost enough to make me laugh if I weren't so transfixed on what's happening between them. And then her hand curls around the tips of my fingers, squeezing with what little strength she has left.

I'm totally and completely fucked.

This woman owns me, and I'm pretty sure she owns Austin as well.

CHAPTER 3

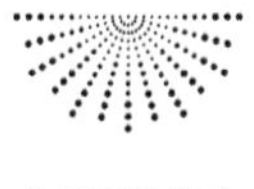

AUSTIN

What the hell am I doing here? I ask myself for the tenth time since walking through the doors of Blackthorne Memorial Hospital.

Flynn elbows me, nudging me forward. I glare at him over my shoulder, rolling my eyes when he smirks at me. He's insufferably upbeat and charming most of the time, but he's my oldest and only friend, far more loyal than a brute like me deserves.

"Nervous?" he teases, though I see a bit of anxiousness in his bright blue eyes.

"No," I lie, facing forward and staring at the door to room 246. *Her* room. The woman I pulled out of the fire.

"Bullshit. You like her."

"Doesn't matter," I grunt, not having the strength to fight him. Besides, he's not wrong. I *do* like her. And I don't like anyone.

It's not just a passing interest or concern for her safety and follow-up care, either. It's...fuck if I know, but I can still feel the weight of her soft, curvy body in my arms when I lifted her off the ground.

Mine, fucking mine, fucking beautiful, pure, sweet goddess...

I rub my temples, trying to quiet the possessive stream of consciousness that's flooded my brain ever since I first held her. I'm used to intrusive thoughts bombarding me at all hours of the day and night, but they've never been directed at another person before.

Normally, my inner monologue veers more toward self-loathing. The voices in my head spit hatred and inconvenient truths, reminding me that my only purpose is to save as many people as I can. The moment I stop being useful, I might as well give up the breath in my lungs. That's the way I see it, anyway.

When I burst into the landing on the third floor of that office building, however, every single insidious thought withered away, replaced with the need to protect the sweet girl fighting for her life amongst the flames.

I've dragged my fair share of people from burning buildings, but saving her was unlike anything I've ever felt. Mainly because of the fact that I felt anything at all. Usually, when I'm on a job, I'm laser focused. Get in, assess, get everyone to safety. Today, though, seeing her terrified green eyes, so determined, so defeated, so completely broken and helpless...

Jesus. I grunt and clear my throat, not sure what to do with these tender emotions leaking their way out of me. For the first time in damn near twenty years, I feel vulnerable. Like I'm wearing my heart around on the outside of my body, just asking the little goddess with green eyes to stomp on it and put me out of my misery.

"Hey," Flynn says, his voice soft and low. "You good?"

I swallow hard and nod my head. If anyone else asked me that or talked to me in that tone of voice, I'd snap their fucking head off. Flynn knows me, though, better than anyone. He's seen the beast I try to keep locked inside; seen the devastation I can bring about when something sets me off. The man even uprooted his life to move out here to Blackthorne Mountain and dragged me with him, kicking and screaming. It turned out to be the best thing for us, though my struggles were far from over.

I hate that I'm such a burden to him, but Flynn won't go away. I've tried brushing him off and convincing him to start a new life without a big ugly monster like me weighing him down, but the man won't take a hint. I'm no good for him, or for anyone. I'm a shitty friend, but Flynn doesn't seem to care.

"Let's just check on her, yeah?" he murmurs. "Make sure she's got family or friends to stay with her for a few days."

I nod my head again, listening to every word he says. Flynn has a calming presence about him, always putting people at ease. Me? Not so much. At six foot eight and two hundred and eighty pounds, there's nothing calming about my presence. Especially my scars. Big, nasty things, scrawled up my arms, chest, and neck.

She wasn't afraid of me, though. My little one. She took one look at me and latched onto my soul.

I heave out a breath and roll my shoulders before quietly knocking on the door. When she doesn't answer, I push it open slightly, unprepared for what lies on the other side.

My sweet girl is curled up in the hospital bed, her light red hair matted to the side of her tear-stained face. Her eyes are closed, her body heavy with sleep. She has a few bandages on her arms from some minor cuts and burns, and an IV drip to keep her hydrated.

The hospital room around her is dim, gray, and unremarkable, but the goddess resting on the bed glows, even in her tarnished state. I watch the subtle rise and fall of her chest, thankful for each new breath she inhales.

I was worried they were going to have to put a trach

down her throat to help her breathe, but it looks like she was able to manage on her own. I knew she was a fighter, through and through. Felt it when I held her trembling body. She was on the edge of giving up. Christ, I know what that's like. I live that reality every damn day. But then her eyes caught mine and I knew. We were both fighting to make it to that moment.

My feet carry me further into the room until I'm right next to her. She's still got a few smudges on her otherwise pale, porcelain skin, and I reach out before I realize what I'm doing. Brushing my fingertips over her stained flesh, I bite back a groan. She's so fucking soft, everywhere.

I trail my fingers down her cheek, tucking some of her hair behind one cute little ear. I didn't know ears could be cute, but everything about this goddess calls to me. I can't seem to pull my hand away from her, the thought of not touching her almost as painful as losing a limb.

My fingertips skim down her throat, pausing briefly to feel her pulse right beneath her ear. God, I've never been more relieved to feel a heartbeat in my life. My hand finds hers, and even though I have no idea what I'm doing, I curl my fingers around her tiny hand and hold it, hoping to somehow reassure her that she'll always be safe from this moment on.

I have no right to promise her these things. Hell, the little lady will probably take one look at me in the cold, hard light of day and run away screaming. I wouldn't blame her. Still, I know somewhere deep down in my gut that I'll never walk away. I'll always be here for her, even if I have to hide in the shadows. I've found my new reason for existing. Her.

And I don't even know her name.

Fucking Brent loaded her up into the ambulance moments after I found her in the parking lot. I wanted to sink my fist into his face and hear the satisfying crunch of bone on bone, but Flynn stepped in and reminded me she needed to get medical attention.

I was agitated, to say the least. Even more so after the ambulance doors slammed shut, taking away the first person to make me feel anything in nearly two decades. Somehow, Flynn knew exactly what was wrong. I have no idea how. I swear sometimes he can read my mind.

He arranged for us to head back early and check in on her since she was the only person inside. It was a severe but neatly contained fire. None of the other floors caught fire. The fire itself is twenty kinds of suspicious, but I don't have the brain capacity to figure it out right now. Not when the soft little goddess is stirring in her sleep.

Her hand twists in mine and she squeezes my fingers, sending a rush of adrenaline surging through me. My knees buckle. I fucking collapse into the chair next to her bed, the strength zapped from my muscles at that one touch.

And then she blinks awake.

My heart stills as I stare down into the green pools of her eyes. I don't even dare to breathe, too afraid I'll scare the beautiful, innocent creature away. Her gaze travels over my face, and I wonder what she sees. My skin is so rough compared to hers, weathered by the harsh life I've lived.

I follow her eyes as they trail over my shoulder and down my arm, settling on where our hands are connected. I jerk back from her, assuming she was offended by my forwardness, but the goddess shocks me by holding on even tighter.

Her pale white, delicate little fingers weave in between my darkened, calloused ones, her touch gentler than anything I've ever experienced in my whole life. I watch in absolute awe as she rubs her thumb over my knuckles, feeling the knotted skin there from countless burns and cuts over the years. I'm not worthy of her tender touch, but I'm powerless to pull away.

My other hand reaches out to do...what? Cup her face? Draw her closer to me so I can consume her sweetness? Fuck no, I don't deserve it. I run my fingers through my hair instead, tugging on the ends roughly and letting the sting ground me.

"How are you feeling?" I grunt out, my voice harsh, almost angry sounding. I squeeze my eyes shut, chastising myself for not knowing how to be soft and patient like Flynn. Speaking of Flynn…

I open my eyes, scanning the room for my best friend. He's supposed to be the buffer between myself and the rest of the world. Talking to people is his deal, not mine. Clearly.

Flynn is standing on the other side of the hospital bed, his arms crossed over his chest and his lips pulled into an amused smirk. The bastard. He winks at me and gives me a slight nod, encouraging me to continue.

"I-I'm f-fine," comes the scratchy, quiet voice of the little goddess next to me.

She drags in a breath but ends up coughing and sputtering for air. I spring into action, needing to end her discomfort as soon as possible. Spotting a glass of water on the table next to her, I try dropping her hand from mine so I can grab it.

"N-no!" comes the choked-out sound. I turn back to the achingly gorgeous woman, nearly collapsing again when I see the fear in her eyes. She claws at my hand, burying her much smaller one inside, as if being apart from me was painful.

"I've got you," I whisper, wrapping both of my hands around hers. She's still shaking and coughing slightly, but the panic is gone from her eyes.

Flynn steps up next to me with the glass of water,

offering it to the woman. Her eyes dart from mine to Flynn's, then back to mine, as if asking if he's trustworthy. It's the kind of look Flynn usually gets from people about me, not the other way around.

"You're safe with us," I tell her, trying to keep my voice low.

"We just wanted to check on you and make sure you're doing alright," Flynn adds, handing her the water again. She accepts it this time, though she keeps one hand wrapped tightly around mine, her fingers squeezing me as if I'm somehow anchoring her.

"Th-thank you," the woman finally says after taking a few sips of water. Her voice is still scratchy from all the smoke inhalation, and I'm sure her throat will be raw for a few days. "I'm...I'm so sorry about the fire," she whispers. "I don't know how it happened or what started it. I swear."

My brow furrows and I find myself rubbing my thumb against the smooth skin on the inside of her wrist. "Don't worry about the fire," I command, wincing once again at the intensity of my voice. I clear my throat and try again. "Your health is the most important thing."

Those green eyes blink up at me, her forehead creasing in confusion. Those pretty pink lips of hers part slightly as if she wants to ask me something. Instead, she chews on her bottom lip and tips her head down, twin spots of red glowing on her cheeks. Holy hell, how is she this goddamn adorable a mere few hours after I pulled her from a burning building?

"Thanks," she murmurs. "I don't know if my boss will see it that way."

"Fuck him," I growl, making the woman jump. *Shit, I have to be careful with her.* "Sorry," I mutter.

She surprises me once again by looking up at me through her lashes, the tiniest hint of a smirk twinkling in her emerald green depths.

"What's your name, beautiful?" Flynn asks, settling into the chair on the other side of the hospital bed.

Without breaking eye contact with me, she whispers, "Tasha."

"Tasha," I repeat just as softly, squeezing her little hand in mine. "I'm Austin."

"And no one asked, but I'm Flynn."

I roll my eyes and Tasha lets out the cutest little giggle. Christ, it hits me square in the chest, knocking the wind right out of me. She's so fucking *pure,* I'm afraid I'm going to dirty her up just by breathing the same air.

Hell, now I'm thinking of all the ways I could dirty up an innocent little creature like Tasha. I haven't been with anyone in...Jesus, I can't remember. Not since we moved out here, that's for sure. Flynn and I have shared women in the past, but only ever as a casual thing. I'm too fucked up to be in a relationship, and Flynn seems content to have the occasional fling, though it's been years since he's even done that much.

There's nothing casual about Tasha. She'd be devastating to have, to hold, to make ours in every way. She'd ruin us for all other women, I can already tell. Once would never be enough.

Not that it matters. God, my thoughts are so far from appropriate. I'm visiting the woman in a hospital after she was in a traumatic fire. What the hell is wrong with me?

"You saved me," she says, breaking into my barbaric thoughts. Her lips are slightly parted like she's in awe. Like I'm her hero. Normally, I'd hate that look. I'm no one's hero. But for Tasha? Hell, I'd do just about anything to keep her from finding out my darkness. I want her to always think of me as her hero. Her protector. "Both of you," she adds, tearing her gaze away from me to look at Flynn.

"Blackthorne Fire Department, at your service, ma'am,"

Flynn teases, giving her his most charming grin. She returns it, though her hand is still wrapped around mine in a tight grip. Does he make her nervous? Do I? I wish I knew what she was thinking.

"Well..." Tasha rubs her lips together, almost like a nervous gesture. She then smooths some of her strawberry blonde hair out of her face, which is still bright red. I'd find her blush as adorable as the rest of her, except she seems embarrassed by it. "Thank you for your service. Or, oh wow, is that what you say to firefighters? I think that's for military people. I'm sorry. I mean, thank you for saving me. And for your service, but not military service. Unless you did serve, in which case...oh my gosh, I'm sorry."

She ends her outburst by trying to hide her face in her free hand. I'm unreasonably happy that she doesn't try to pull her other hand away from mine. Instead, she clings to me even harder, like she wants me to make her embarrassment go away. Doesn't she know she never has to feel shame around us?

"Hey," Flynn says, using that calming tone of his. "We're just glad we got to you in time and that no one else was inside."

Tasha lifts her head slightly to look at him. He smiles at her, causing her to blush again, but at least this time she smiles, too. When she turns and looks at me over her shoulder, I barely resist the urge to crawl into the bed and curl myself around her body. She's precious. Priceless. So fucking beautiful and sweet and everything I don't deserve.

"Thank you," she says again, her cheeks burning scarlet. "I don't know what happened. One minute I was in the breakroom reading an article about naked mole rats, and the next minute there was smoke and flames and..."

She shudders, causing me to crouch on the edge of her bed and pull her into my arms. The bed creaks under my weight, but there's no way in hell I'm moving. Not with all of her curvy perfection pressed against me.

"You don't have to talk about it," I murmur onto the top of her head. Her hair still smells like smoke, but she's overwhelmingly sweet, like peaches and cream. Addicting. She smells addicting. Tasha nods against my chest and I lean back, adjusting us so we're lying in the hospital bed.

I look over at Flynn, who has a smug smirk on his stupid face. He settles back in his chair and props his feet up on the edge of the bed, lacing his fingers together behind his head and reclining. He looks like a cocky son of a bitch who knows something I don't.

"Get some rest, Tasha," he says soothingly. "We'll hang out for a bit."

"I'm sorry," she whispers, tipping her head up to look at me. God, those eyes. Wide, trusting, brimming with tears, and so damn vulnerable I want to wrap her up in my arms and never let her go. "I d-don't know why I'm c-crying."

"I've got you," I manage to say, cupping the back of her neck and massaging it lightly. "You've been through a lot." I don't know where these soft-spoken words are coming from, but she seems to appreciate them. Tasha nods her head as the first tear spills down her cheek. I somehow know her tears are for what she's been through, and not just for today.

I gently tuck her head under my chin and Flynn helps me pull the blankets up. Tasha lets out a deep breath, relaxing into me as I stretch my hand out over her back, rubbing up and down in soothing strokes.

Flynn inhales sharply, and I turn to look at him. Tasha is holding onto the very tips of his fingers, even as she buries her face further into my chest like she needs both of us to keep her grounded.

My eyes meet Flynn's, his blue irises sparking with something I've never seen before. "She's perfect," he mouths silently. I grunt and nod my head once, not sure what to do about the protective, possessive feelings flooding through every cell in my body.

She's perfect. Perfect. Perfect for us.

How the hell did this happen?

CHAPTER 4

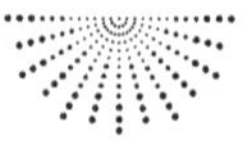

TASHA

I slowly stand up from where I'm perched on the edge of the hospital bed, taking time to stretch out my sore limbs. Every muscle aches and my throat feels impossibly scratchy and dry, but overall, I'm incredibly lucky to be alive.

The doctor just handed me my paperwork and told me I could leave. I gather my torn, charred clothes and shove them in the plastic bag one of the nurses gave me earlier this morning when she woke me up, along with a pair of scrubs and slip-on shoes to wear home.

I don't remember much of the last few days I've spent here. I was mostly sleeping and drinking water. However, I certainly remember my visitors on that first night. Austin and Flynn. The two men who saved me. I can't believe they came to visit me in the hospital. I'm a nobody.

Flynn had bright blue eyes that sparkled when he smiled. His light brown hair was a bit of a mess on top of his head, but in that effortlessly sexy way that I thought was only possible on magazine covers and in movies.

And his body...I'm embarrassed to admit I even noticed in the first place. I mean, it's totally inappropriate. But his lean muscles and confident stride made parts of me ache that have never ached before. He didn't say much, but his presence was enough. I felt safe with him and a small part of me appreciated the distance he kept because my God... Austin was a force to be reckoned with.

He was intense. Commanding. All consuming. I felt everything about Austin as soon as he walked into my hospital room yesterday before I even opened my eyes. Flynn is tall, broad, and muscular, but Austin is on a whole other level. The man is huge, corded with muscles, tattoos, and scars. When he skimmed the very tips of his fingers over my cheek, I felt a piece of his tortured soul scrape against mine.

As impossible as it still is to believe, the intimidatingly large, rough firefighter felt fragile when I wrapped my hand around his. Like he was about to break, and I somehow helped hold him together with my touch.

That's not the entire reason I couldn't seem to slip my hand from his, though. I needed him as much as he needed me. Whatever happened when those dark brown eyes locked onto mine for the first time, we were both feeling it. Raw. Exposed. Torn apart for the other to see, if only for a few moments.

And then I went and coughed and made a fool of myself, thanking them for their service. What the heck is wrong with me? As if that weren't enough, I stuttered my way through a pathetic explanation of the fire, probably not making one lick of sense the entire time. And then I ugly-cried all over Austin until I passed out from exhaustion.

My temples pound unevenly, the painful pressure building and building until a tension headache flares behind my eyes. I'm such an embarrassing idiot. Flynn and Austin were just doing their duty. I'm sure I warped whatever comfort they were willing to provide into a much bigger deal than it was.

I must have, otherwise wouldn't they still be here?

But of course, I'm being silly. I mean, Blackthorne is a small town. The two men were just checking in on the awkward loner who may or may not have started a fire in her office building. I'm the one who went and made things awkward by curling up underneath the blankets with Austin while holding Flynn's hand.

Shameful tears burn in the back of my eyes. I know I'll be replaying every embarrassing moment of our interaction later on tonight when I'm trying to sleep. What was I thinking, touching them like that?

I try to do a breathing exercise to help calm my racing thoughts, but my lungs still ache. At least today is Saturday. I'll have the weekend to somewhat recover before returning to the office on Monday.

Oh, God.

I squeeze my hands into fists, fighting off the wave of anxiety threatening to drown me. On Monday I'll have to face everyone. I already talked to the cops this morning. They were nice enough, even though I blubbered my way through the whole thing. I'm not sure if they believed that it wasn't my fault, but they didn't arrest me, so that has to be a good sign.

"There you are, beautiful." Flynn's bright, yet soothing voice filters into the room, loosening the tight band around my chest ever so slightly. I hear him walk closer, each step banishing the wave of anxiety until it's mostly receded.

"Um, hi," I squeak out, clutching the plastic bag full of my clothes against my chest as I turn to face him. *Does he really think I'm beautiful?*

Those blue eyes shine down on me, making me feel warm and welcome, if only for a few brief moments. I can't look away as he closes the distance between us. Flynn slowly reaches out toward me, gently brushing a few strands of hair behind my ear. I'm sure I look like a greasy, matted mess, but I strangely don't feel embarrassed. How can I when he's looking at me like I'm some rare treasure?

"Did the doc get your discharge papers already?"

"Oh, um, yes, how did you…?"

"I've called every morning and evening to ask for updates," Flynn answers my unfinished question with an easy confidence. I'm speechless, but Flynn continues. "We wanted to come see you again, but Austin and I have had a long couple of shifts. Anyway, Doc Gracen said you'd be discharged this afternoon, so here I am."

Flynn's lips turn up into a grin, one that I feel all the way down to the tips of my toes. I sway closer to him without even realizing it, wanting to soak up more of his sweet smile and comforting presence. He wraps an arm around me, tucking me into his side as if it's the most natural thing in the world.

"Um, where...where are we going?" I ask dumbly as he leads us out into the hallway. "I-I don't have a car here," I stutter out like an idiot. Of course, he knows my car isn't here. He saw me get loaded up into an ambulance.

"Good thing I do," Flynn replies, squeezing me a little bit tighter before loosening his hold again. "I'm taking you home. The doc let me know you're all alone in your apartment."

"Oh." It's barely a whisper. I'm not even sure Flynn heard my response. Of course he's being nice to me. He knows I'm a loser with no one to give me a ride home. "I can manage to get home okay on my own," I tell him.

"I'm taking you to my place. I live with Austin up on Blackthorne mountain. You can—"

"What?!" I say it so forcefully, a cough rattles loose from deep in my chest. Flynn rubs my back and pulls a water bottle from a backpack I didn't notice he was holding. I take a few swigs, trying to get my breathing under control. *What the heck is happening here?*

"It'll just be for a few days," Flynn continues without missing a beat. He says it so easily, as if it's not weird at all for him to invite a stranger into his home after only knowing them for a handful of hours. Then again, maybe it isn't. I don't know anything about him or Austin.

“No, th-thank you,” I mutter, getting some of my wits about me. “I'll be fine. I...I have to water my plants.” It sounds lame, but it's true. It's part of my Saturday morning routine, which I'm now already four hours behind on. I talk to my plants and give them breakfast. Then I have coffee on my loveseat while reading two chapters of whatever book I'm into at the time. After a shower and throwing a load in the laundry, Saturdays are spent cleaning and organizing. It's not an exciting life, but it's familiar and mine and I'm comfortable with how I have things set up.

“We can water your plants, beautiful,” Flynn says softly, turning his kind blue eyes to focus on mine. “And I'll make your coffee so you can read three chapters if you want. I'll help with laundry. You probably shouldn't be doing too much cleaning today, though.”

My eyes go wide when I realize I must have said all of that out loud. *What is wrong with me?* Before I can spiral too much, Flynn rests his hand on my shoulder, silently, softly bringing me back into the moment with him.

“Hey,” he says so gently I feel stupid tears pricking my eyes again. “Everything is going to be alright, sweetheart. You've been through so much, let me take care of you. Just for the weekend,” he adds when I don't say anything.

“Why?”

Flynn's hand on my shoulder slowly moves to cup the side of my neck, his thumb gently caressing the underside of my chin. His gaze is so tender, so full of emotion I almost have to look away.

"I get the sense you've been taking care of yourself for a long time now," he murmurs, those clear blue eyes peering down into the core of me. I can't look away and I find I don't want to. "Let me do it for a little while," he says so softly I *feel* more than hear his words.

"Okay." It slips right out of my mouth, but I don't dare take it back. I have no idea why this ridiculously handsome, charming man feels compelled to make sure I'm okay, but I'm too tired to fight it. "But I can't stay over at your house," I add, nodding firmly. *Go me! Way to assert dominance!*

Flynn smiles, his lips parting to reveal straight, white teeth. His eyes light up and he pulls me closer into his side before dropping a kiss on top of my head. What is happening here? Is this part of his thing? Giving sweet kisses and smiling so broadly it makes my knees weak?

"I'll take you to your place then, beautiful. As long as you let me pamper you for the day, I'll be happy."

I'm left speechless once again, but I nod and let him lead me out to his truck.

Ten minutes later, we're pulling up to my apartment. It's not the biggest or most well-maintained building in town, but it's better than some of the places I lived growing up. I never thought I'd have company, but now that Flynn is here, I'm starting to look at everything more critically.

The siding could use a good power wash and a fresh coat of paint, and the security leaves a bit to be desired. The sidewalk leading up to my front door is cracked in several places and the side railing is more rust than metal.

Still, it's mine. I fought hard to have a space of my own, and I've never been prouder than when I was first handed my keys.

Shoot. My keys. My phone. All my stuff. I left everything in the office the day of the fire. How could I forget?

"Mrs. Fonda said she put a spare key under your mat," Flynn says, startling me. He's already parked right in front of my unit, hopped out, and opened my door for me. I stare down at him in confusion. Can he read my mind?

"How do you know my landlord?"

Flynn holds out his hand to help me climb out of his truck. I stumble a bit when my foot hits the ground, and my big, strong firefighter pulls me into his arms, steadying me while he looks me up and down.

"I called this morning," he says after a few moments of just staring at me. "Explained the situation and asked for a spare key. I'm sure if she didn't know both me and my ma, she wouldn't have told me where she put it."

"Oh." I'm shocked he went through the effort to take care of a detail like that. "I...thank you, Flynn. I don't know what I would have done without you. I don't even have my phone," I ramble to myself.

"Never thank me, beautiful," he says with the most genuine smile. "But that reminds me…" Flynn reaches past me and digs around in the center console of his truck before handing me a phone. "It's an older iPhone, but it still works. I wiped it clean this morning and added you to our phone plan. It doesn't have to be permanent, but I didn't like the thought of you not having a way to communicate. Of course, I hoped you'd come stay the weekend so Austin and I could keep an eye on you, but I understand your hesitation. And...well, anyway."

Flynn shrugs, and oh my gosh, are the tips of his ears red? Is he blushing?

"This is…"

"Not much, I know. We can get you an upgrade. Whatever you want."

"Flynn," I whisper, clutching his hand with mine and squeezing. I can't help it. My words aren't there. "Thank you," I manage to choke out.

"What did I say about thanking me?" he murmurs, squeezing my hand right back. "My number is in there, as well as Austin's. What else do you need?"

A hug?

Of course, I don't say that. "I'm good, really. This is too much. I'll just keep it until I can afford another one. Oh crap," I whisper. Speaking of money and affording things, my purse with my cash, cards, and ID. Dammit, so many little things I don't have the energy to do anything about right now.

"Let's get you inside," Flynn says, giving my hand one last squeeze before letting go. I nod numbly, thinking about all the calls I'll have to make and bills I'll have to switch over.

With a hand at the small of my back, my handsome firefighter guides me up the three porch stairs to my door, retrieving the key for me and letting me do the honors. Something about that makes me feel all warm and tingly inside. He wanted me to have the final say on whether he comes in or not.

I push the door open and look over my shoulder, nodding my head and letting him know I want him here. Why, I'm not sure, but I don't like the thought of being alone after what I've just been through. Normally, I'd want nothing more than to crawl under my blankets and hide out from the world. The only thing better might be if Flynn were under them with me, holding me close and protecting me from the world.

That's crazy talk, though. Especially since I fell asleep curled up in Austin's arms a few nights ago. God, what is going on with me? It must be the aftereffects of the fire and my stay in the hospital. I'm wired and jittery and yet completely exhausted.

Flynn steps up behind me, wrapping his solid arm around my hips and guiding me inside. I can walk just fine, but I don't mind the excuse to be closer to him. His sandalwood scent wraps around me as he presses me further into his side. Warm, hard muscles flex against my curves, and I ignore the spark sizzling between my thighs.

What the hell?

He sets me down on my small loveseat and then crouches down in front of me, resting his hands on my knees. "How are you feeling, beautiful? What can I get you?"

It takes me a second to register his question. I'm too busy counting the shades of blue in his eyes and trying to figure out why I want to crawl into his lap and let him rock me to sleep.

"Um…I should probably call my bank," I manage to say, reeling in the crazy thoughts.

"I stopped by Blackthorne Bank this morning before picking you up. I figured it was a safe bet you banked there since it's the only one in town." I nod, confirming his suspicions, though I'm not sure where he's going with this. "I obviously have no control over your finances, but I did tell the bank manager about the fire and that you probably lost your purse and wallet. They can have a new card sent to you as soon as you call, but there's no rush. Just rest up today, you don't have to worry about anything."

"Is that standard firefighter protocol?" I ask.

Flynn smiles, his crystal blue eyes shining with mischief. "For you? Absolutely. I also talked to your boss."

"You did?" I gasp, immediately chewing on my lip. That was the one thing I was dreading most. Calling Harry.

Flynn nods. "He's kind of a prick."

This startles a laugh out of me, which of course turns into a cough. Flynn jumps up and gets me a glass of water, sprinting back to me. I take a few grateful sips, trying to collect my thoughts. "What...what did he say?"

Flynn furrows his brow, his eyes studying my features. "Nothing to worry about, beautiful," he murmurs, softening his face into a smile. "You get paid time off next week. Workplace injury and all that." I'm about to protest, but Flynn must see it coming. "No arguments. It's company policy." Again, I open my mouth to ask how he knows about my company policy, but Flynn continues. "Anyway, we can go over the details later. Right now you need lunch."

"So do you," I say, practically pouting. My response surprises me as much as Flynn, who chuckles. "I-I just mean you've been running around doing errands for me and cleaning up my mess. If anyone deserves lunch, it's you."

Those blue eyes change to a slightly darker color as he tilts his head to the side. Flynn opens and closes his mouth a few times before finally responding. "It's no trouble, Tasha. I like doing these things, especially for you."

Especially for me? What does that mean?

"I run errands for Austin, too, but that bastard never thanks me." Flynn rolls his eyes, but I see the love he has for Austin all the same. "And no one is more deserving to be taken care of than you, sweetheart. You've had a rough couple of days."

"But..."

"Pizza should be here any minute. I wasn't sure what you liked, so I got half cheese, half pepperoni."

"Flynn, I don't have any money, remember?"

"And I'm taking care of you today, remember?"

"But..."

"No buts," he says with a wink, just as the doorbell rings.

"But who takes care of you?"

I didn't mean to say it out loud, but the words must have slipped out. Flynn freezes, his gaze flittering around my face until it rests heavily on my eyes. I'm not sure what's going on in his head, but it seems the man with all the answers is speechless for once.

The doorbell rings again, jarring him out of his daze. Flynn gives me his most charming grin and grabs the pizza, paying the delivery guy and thanking him. Whatever moment of vulnerability that passed between us is over, and he's back to being his confident, charismatic self.

Still, as we eat slice after slice of pizza, I can't get that look out of my mind. He seemed so...lonely. That can't be right, though. I'm sure someone like Flynn has tons of friends and plenty of women to warm his bed at night.

I ignore that nasty knot of jealousy in the pit of my stomach once more, focusing instead on Flynn and the story he's telling me about Austin and him as kids. I have no idea how long I'll have Flynn in my life, let alone my apartment, but I want to remember every moment.

CHAPTER 5

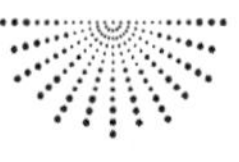

FLYNN

"Well?" Austin growls from the kitchen of our cabin.

"Well, what?" I ask, not even trying to hide my smirk. I know exactly what he really wants to say to me. He's been grumpier than usual since he got home from his shift at the fire station.

"How is she?" he grunts, banging around the kitchen to avoid having an actual conversation with me.

"Jealous I got to spend time alone with her?" I tease. Austin growls, his jaw tensing as he stares a hole through my head. I hold my hands up in surrender, grinning at his over-the-top reaction. Tasha has the broody giant all twisted up and she has no idea. Both of us are ready to drop to our knees for her.

Fuck, I'd get on my knees for her every day. Push her skirt up her shapely legs and bury my face between her thighs...

Austin slams a cupboard door shut, rattling the damn thing on its hinges. "Just tell me she's okay," he mutters, making his way into the living room to sit across from me. I feel like a jerk for joking around once I see the haunted look in his eyes. It's clear Austin hasn't thought of anything other than our girl all day, and here I am, rubbing it in that I had the day off to spend spoiling her, just like I promised.

"She's a fighter," I tell him seriously. "I tried convincing her to stay here with us for the weekend, but it sort of sent her into a tailspin." Austin grunts and nods, looking right at me as if waiting for me to continue. Ever the conversationalist. "She wanted to be in her own space to water her plants."

"She should bring them here," he grunts. "We have space. And sunlight. And water." The determined look in his dark brown eyes makes me chuckle. Typical Austin. Once he decides something, it's automatically the best thing. I think he's about to have his world shaken up for the better when it comes to Tasha.

"It's not really about the plants. She likes things to be a certain way," I continue when it's clear Austin is clueless. "I could tell it was hard for her to deviate from her normal Saturday routine. I mean, the woman has a weekly meal plan laminated and hanging on her fridge, for Christ's sake," I say with a little laugh. It was adorable and impressive at the same time. Every detail was planned out down to the leftovers she would pack for her lunches for the week.

"It's a good idea," Austin huffs, immediately coming to her defense. It only makes me laugh harder.

"Of course it is," I agree, nodding my head. "I'm just saying, we'll have to be careful not to rush her into anything. I think it's important for her to be in control." I got the sense our girl didn't have a very stable childhood. Not that she told me much when I tried asking her personal questions.

Austin furrows his brow and opens his mouth before closing it again. I know he wants to ask what we're rushing her into, but the question dies on his tongue. He knows. He's just not sure what to do about it yet.

"The chief did the final walk-through today," my best friend grunts, changing the subject abruptly. I'd expect nothing less. He leans back in his chair, settling in to tell me about the report on the office fire. "All signs point to arson, but we can't find an accelerant. Or a motive, for that matter. Plus, Tasha was one of three people in the building at the time. The other two were working the front reception desk and ran out at the first sign of trouble."

I lean forward, resting my elbows on my knees. I know Tasha isn't responsible for the fire. The cops who talked to her feel the same way, thank God, otherwise things could get ugly between the firefighters and the police.

Before I get a chance to ask him any questions, my phone rings.

"Hey, beautiful," I answer, darting my eyes to Austin. His features soften when he realizes who I'm talking to.

"F-Flynn?" Tasha's tentative voice makes every one of my muscles tense. She sounds scared. Fuck that, she sounds terrified.

"What's wrong, baby?" I ask, jumping up from the couch. Austin stands as well, looking around the living room until he spots the keys to my truck on one of the side tables. He grabs them and tilts his head toward the front door. I nod, following him outside while I listen to Tasha.

"I...I'm sorry. It's nothing. I'm sure it's nothing. It's nothing," she repeats more to herself than to me.

"What's going on?" I try asking again, making my voice as soft as possible even though I feel the adrenaline coursing through my veins and jacking up my heart rate.

"I thought…" she trails off and then sighs heavily. "Oh, gosh, I thought I saw someone hanging around outside my window. But now that I say it out loud, it sounds ridiculous. I'm just being paranoid. I guess I'm still a little shaken up," she murmurs.

"Your safety is not ridiculous," I tell her as I get into the passenger side of my truck. Austin slams the driver's side door shut and starts the engine. "And that includes how safe you *feel* in your own home, sweetheart."

Austin grunts in agreement, gripping the steering wheel as he navigates down the mountain.

"I feel so silly," Tasha whispers, tears evident in her voice. "I'm fine. Really. I don't know why...I don't know...I'm sorry," she stutters out. "*Ohmygod,*" she mutters under her breath. *"I'm so awkward."*

I'd smile at how endearing she is, but my gut is twisted into a tight ball of rage and worry just thinking about her in her ground floor apartment while some creep is hanging around outside. I also hate that she's so easily embarrassed. Soon our girl will feel safe and comfortable enough to tell us anything. I just have to be patient.

"Take a slow, deep breath for me, Tasha," I tell her, following along with her as she does. Out of the corner of my eye, I see Austin inhaling as well, the three of us connected on some level I don't understand yet. "Austin and I will be there soon."

"What? No, no, God, I'm...you don't have to do that."

"Did you end up finishing your book after I left?" I ask, hoping to keep her talking until we get there.

"Um, yeah, actually," she murmurs. "I should have left some for tomorrow, though," she laments, letting me distract her for the moment. "I have the next book in the series on hold when it comes back to the library, but that won't be until next week. What am I going to do all day tomorrow?"

Her tone is soft and curious, and only a little bit tentative. I know she likes her routines, but hopefully, she's starting to see it's okay to let go every once in a while.

I keep her chatting for the next ten minutes as Austin drives through our small mountain town. I direct him to her apartment, both of us tensing as we approach, hyperaware of our surroundings. I scan the parking lot for signs of anyone in the shadows, relieved but still apprehensive when I don't see anything.

"We're here, beautiful," I tell her as Austin puts the truck in park.

"Oh," she gasps softly. "I…"

"We just want to make sure you're okay," I'm quick to follow up, not wanting her to doubt herself or send us away.

"Yeah," Tasha breathes out. "Yeah, okay."

Thirty seconds later, she swings the door open and steps aside, letting Austin and me into her space. I can tell it took every ounce of courage she had to let us come inside and disrupt her nightly routine. Then again, her night was already stolen from her by whatever scared her in the first place.

Tasha closes the door, taking a measured breath before turning around. Her strawberry blonde hair is piled on top of her head in a messy bun, a few wisps curling around her temples and neck. Her cheeks are flushed and she nibbles on her bottom lip before rubbing her lips together in that nervous gesture of hers.

I want to wrap her up in my arms and tell her she has nothing to be anxious about when we're here. That would be too much too soon, though, and the last thing I want to do is scare my sweet girl away.

She's wearing a thin T-shirt and fuzzy blue sleep shorts that I suddenly want to rub every inch of my hardening cock against. Tasha looks from me to Austin, craning her neck way back to take us in.

We don't exactly fit in her studio apartment, but I'd sleep in a cardboard box if it somehow made Tasha feel safe. I look over at Austin, cracking a smile when I see him hunch his shoulders to try and make himself seem less intimidating. He's so far gone for our girl, and he's hardly even aware of it.

"Uh...water?" Tasha squeaks out, her face turning scarlet

as she clears her throat. “Can I get you guys some water?” she asks again, a little bit more confident this time.

“How are you feeling?” Austin blurts out, his words falling all over hers. God, these two. It’s a good thing they have me.

“I’ll get us some water, beautiful,” I say with my most disarming grin. “Why don’t you show Austin around?”

Tasha rewards me with the cutest little smile, a spark of playfulness catching fire in her green eyes. Holy hell, I can’t breathe when she looks at me like that.

"I don't know if I'll have enough time to give him the grand tour," she teases, sweeping her arm out toward the room. There's a mattress and a box spring in one corner of the room, a loveseat on the other side, and a bookshelf overflowing with paperbacks in between. Her kitchen is about two feet by five feet, complete with a hot plate and a mini fridge. The only door is off to the side of the kitchen, where a tiny bathroom lies in shadows.

“I like it,” Austin grunts, his eyes never leaving her. I roll my eyes and Tasha giggles, the airy sound filling my lungs and making me smile.

“Thanks,” she murmurs, slipping past Austin and walking further into her studio apartment. “Feel free to sit anywhere.”

I quickly grab some water for us and return, smirking when I see Austin folding himself onto her tiny couch. Tasha is standing next to him, looking like she wants to sit on his lap but too afraid to make the first move. That's okay. It'll take time, but eventually, our girl will tell us exactly what she wants and when she wants it. I can't fucking wait.

I’m about to set our waters down on her little side table when the bush outside her window rustles, a few branches scraping against the glass. Tasha flinches and gasps, immediately reaching for Austin’s hand. She grips it so tightly her knuckles turn white.

Austin cups both of her hands in his, just like he did in the hospital. Also just like that day, Tasha relaxes ever so much, trusting Austin to keep her safe.

I make my way to the window, peering out from the corner of her curtains. The bush shakes slightly, and I'm about to fling the door open and start punching it blindly. But then a family of squirrels dashes out from underneath the thick foliage.

"Just some squirrels," I announce, scanning the parking lot to make sure I didn't miss anything.

"Of course," Tasha whispers. "I'm sorry I'm so jumpy."

"There's no need to apologize, sweetheart," I reassure her.

"We can stay the night," Austin suddenly interjects. "If...if you want. To make you feel safe. Protect you from stuff."

"Stuff like squirrels?" Tasha jokes, her voice soft but so damn sweet. Austin has zero charm, but it seems to be working for our girl. She's perfect for us.

"Anything. Everything," Austin vows solemnly, his eyes never leaving hers.

"Well...I..." She's searching for an excuse, but the way her hand never leaves Austin's and her eyes hardly part from mine, I know she wants us to be here as much as we want to be here. "I don't have much in the way of entertainment. I'm kind of boring. Most nights I heat up dinner, clean up a bit, take a shower, brush my teeth, braid my hair, and curl up with a good book."

"You're anything but boring," I insist, taking a few steps closer and wrapping my pinkie finger around hers. Tasha is still holding onto Austin like he's a lifeline, but she lets me touch her, too, so gently. I'm reminded once again of how fragile she is. Strong and brave as fuck, no doubt, but still so delicate.

"I want to see your braided hair," Austin blurts out. He groans a second later and rubs a hand down his face. I chuckle while Tasha laughs.

"I suppose it would be okay for you both to stay. Just for the night. I don't think it'll be very comfortable, though. I just have the bed and the loveseat. I don't have an extra blanket or anything." She mutters something under her breath, and I get the sense she's saying bad things about herself. We'll have to have a talk about that soon, but for now, I'm content that she agreed to let us stay.

Austin and I try to make ourselves comfortable and end up sitting on the floor while Tasha goes through her nightly routine. It's sweet torture listening to the shower turn on and picturing the water dripping down her breasts, her stomach, between her thighs…

"You're still here," Tasha's voice breaks into my dirty thoughts. She sounds shocked. Our girl is dressed in a tank top with another pair of sleep shorts. They look silky and have the cutest clouds dotted all over them. Her hair is woven into a perfect braid, resting over one shoulder. She's sweet, innocent perfection. And Christ, I want to feast on every inch of her.

"There's nowhere else we'd rather be," I tell her, reigning in my lustful thoughts.

"Okay then," she murmurs, her cheeks flushing the cutest shade of pink. "Like I said, it won't be very comfortable. I suppose one of you...if you wanted to, I mean...one of you could sleep up here with me." She rushes to say the last part, tossing the words out there and then wincing.

Every muscle in my body freezes and my heart stutters inside my chest. Christ almighty, I want it to be me. But I know it needs to be Austin. They need this.

"It's only fair the big brute gets the bed," I say, nudging Austin with my foot. He's silent and still; I swear he's not even breathing. "I can fold myself onto the couch, but Austin? Not so much."

I kick him a little harder, and this time he springs up off

the floor. "Yeah," he says eagerly before trying to cover it with a cough. I bite back a laugh at the big oaf. Tasha presses her lips together, trying and failing to hide a smile.

I scoot the loveseat closer to the bed as Tasha climbs in. Austin crawls in behind Tasha, his movements tentative and unsteady. He panics at first, but then something incredible happens. Tasha reaches behind her and finds his arm, tugging it around her waist. The giant of a man melts against her sweetness, tucking her further into his chest as he curls around her.

She's good for him.

I let that thought settle deep in my gut as I shut off the little lamp next to the couch and get situated for the night. I find a semi-comfortable position with my feet propped up on the corner of the mattress. Truthfully, it doesn't matter much. I know I won't sleep a wink tonight.

Tasha shuffles slightly underneath the blanket, and then I see her hand slide out from the edge, slowly reaching out toward mine. I stay still, not wanting to scare her away. The most I can hope for is a little squeeze on the tips of my fingers like she's done the last two days.

My sweet, beautiful girl gives me the greatest gift ever. She laces our fingers together, clinging to me and infusing her warmth. She's touching my goddamn soul, setting it ablaze with that one simple move.

She rubs her lips together, the movement barely visible in the moonlight coming in through her one window. "What are you thinking about?" I murmur, wanting to know everything about her.

"I feel so safe," she whispers, answering me instantly. I love that she's getting more comfortable speaking her truth around us.

"You are," I promise. I lift her hand, turning it slightly so I can kiss the inside of her wrist. My lips brush against her pulse, beating rapidly just beneath her skin.

Austin grunts his agreement, and I barely suppress my eye roll. The man will need to learn how to use his words one of these days.

Tasha's eyes sparkle with laughter, bright enough to see even in the mostly dark room. She looks at me like we're sharing an inside joke, like all three of us have been together for far longer than a few days.

"Thank you," she sighs contentedly, snuggling deeper into her blankets. Austin tightens his hold on her, burying his face into the top of her head. I long to do the same, but for now, it's enough to see the two of them together.

"Anything for you, sweetheart."

Tasha's eyes flutter closed and she's asleep within moments. A fierce pride roars through me, knowing we soothed her fears enough to fall asleep so fast. I look behind her, my gaze meeting Austin's.

He looks like the strangest mix of contentment and complete shock. "What are we doing?" he mouths, looking at where I'm holding her hand.

"Loving her," I answer simply, smirking when he gawks at me. "Go ahead. Tell me I'm wrong."

After a long stretch of silence, I smile to myself, completely satisfied with how well things are progressing. Hopefully, she'll be in our bed soon.

CHAPTER 6

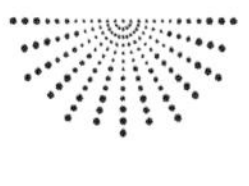

AUSTIN

I grunt my thanks to the barista, collecting the five dollar sugary beverage and heading out to my car. I'd never touch this stuff, but Tasha told Flynn and me she sometimes splurges on caramel vanilla lattes with extra whipped cream, but that it's been a while.

I decided she deserves her favorite drink more than occasionally, so here I am, getting fancy coffee and looking up directions to the nearest floral shop. Luckily, there's one a few blocks away.

Pulling into the parking lot, I hop out of my car and jog up to the door, relieved to see they are open. I'm not sure what Tasha likes, or what any woman likes, for that matter. I've never bought flowers for anyone before. I have no idea what I'm doing.

The lady behind the counter takes pity on me and suggests a few arrangements. I don't know anything about flowers, but I go for the biggest bouquet, selecting a vase to match.

Ten minutes later, I'm parked in front of her place,

rubbing my sweaty palms on my jeans and trying to calm down.

It's been two days since I've seen our girl. Damn Flynn kept calling her that and I guess it stuck. Someone as pure, sweet, and shy as Tasha couldn't ever truly belong to a mangled beast like me, but for some reason, she likes having me around.

When I woke up Sunday morning with Tasha wrapped around me, I never wanted to leave. Her curvy little body was draped over mine and my arms were locked around her waist, holding her close.

God, I can still smell her sweet peaches and cream scent from when I greedily buried my nose into her hair and breathed her in. It took every damn thing in me to peel her off my chest, but I had to stop by the station and check in on a few things before my shift started that night. Plus, if I stayed there any longer, I might have flipped her on her back and begged her to let me fuck her tits.

But that would have been barbaric and totally inappropriate.

So, I settled on filling my lungs with her scent and pressing the softest kiss to her temple before sneaking out of bed. I told Flynn what was up and he promised to look after her again. He had a few days off, and now it's my turn. Flynn started his shift at the fire station last night while I finally have the day off. I'm not wasting a single second.

Throwing the door of my car open, I grab the coffee and flowers and head up to Tasha's front door. I stand there like an idiot, both of my hands full and unable to knock on the door. Shuffling the coffee and giant vase of flowers around, I manage to awkwardly balance them enough to free a hand to knock.

I listen intently, my heart pounding painfully against my ribcage. A few moments of silence pass and I wonder if she's home. Where else would she be? She's still recovering from her traumatic experience and she's said herself she doesn't go out much.

Then I hear her shuffling around, though it sounds like she's moving rather slowly. I pull out my phone, cursing when I see how early it is. Seven am on a Tuesday morning. *She was probably asleep, asshole.*

Dammit, I'm already fucking this up.

I hear her just on the other side of the door, and then a shadow falls over the little peephole. She gasps and flings the door open, blinking up at me in surprise. She's so soft and sweet and sleepy, her heavy eyelids drooping as she stifles a yawn.

"Austin," she breathes out, her pink lips curling into the cutest, shiest smile.

"Little one," I murmur, my heart fucking melting at the sight of her. She blushes at my name for her, and I barely resist the urge to kiss her rosy cheeks.

"Oh wow, is that all for me?" she asks, her eyes wandering to the flowers and coffee. I realize now how obnoxious the flowers are. Tacky even. And the coffee is probably cold.

I nod and swallow the lump in my throat, feeling like even more of an idiot with my pathetic offering. "Yeah, but I can—"

"Come in," she rushes to say, swinging the door open and stepping aside. I get my first good look at her in days, and she's somehow more gorgeous, more precious, more *everything* than I remember. Especially in her little nightgown.

Fuck me, it's not overtly sexual, more of a baggy shirt than anything else, but the way it hangs off her curves and hits mid-thigh makes me want to rip it off of her and suck every inch of her creamy skin.

I stumble forward, still trying to balance everything in my arms. I take a few steps inside, toward her little bedside table, attempting to set the coffee and heavy vase down. I watch in slow motion as the coffee starts to slip from my grip. I clutch it tighter, only to crush the flimsy paper cup in my hand and spray lukewarm liquid all over her bed and carpet.

"Shit, I'm sorry," I growl, quickly setting the empty cup down along with the flowers. I turn on my heel, hoping to grab a towel to help her clean up, but I bump the table with my foot, kicking the leg of the rickety thing clean off.

I watch in horror as the vase wobbles and falls to the ground, shattering and spilling water and flowers all over the place, not to mention glass.

"Fuck," I grunt, falling to my knees to try and somehow salvage this situation. Looking around me, though, I know I've destroyed her place and upset her whole routine. Our girl likes to stick to a schedule. She's neat and tidy and orderly. And here I am, barging in first thing in the morning and ruining her safe haven.

I can't look at her. Tasha hasn't said anything this whole time, and I'm guessing she's trying to figure out how to politely kick me out.

Fucking screw up. You ruined her day and damaged her property. You're not good enough for her. You're not meant for a relationship.

My racing thoughts bombard me, filling my head with sinister whispers and reminding me that I don't deserve to be in Tasha's presence. I can feel my heart hammering in my chest, feel each palpitation as it pumps heated blood through my veins.

Balling my hands into tight fists, I squeeze my eyes shut and try to think of a way to escape. I feel the darkness clouding my mind, my shameful rage building with each ragged breath. I don't want my precious goddess to see me like this. I never want her to be exposed to the monster I try to keep locked up inside.

The lightest touch on my hand quells the burning self-hatred. I don't open my eyes or even dare to breathe, too afraid I'll scare my little one away. She wraps her hand around my clenched up fist, her thumb rubbing back and forth over my knuckles.

"It's okay," she whispers soothingly. Her breath brushes against my cheek, the warmth of her body next to mine almost more than I can take. Why is she so good to me? So patient and understanding, even though I'm the last person who deserves her kindness.

"I'm sorry," I choke out, the words coming out harsh and jagged. "I...I..."

Tasha stands up, and I feel the loss of her immediately. This is what I was waiting for—her to see who I really am and leave me. Then she shocks the hell out of me by tugging on my hand, urging me to stand with her.

Slowly, I open my eyes, looking up into the green gaze of my little one. With the early morning sunlight illuminating the room, she looks absolutely ethereal, like an angel of mercy, like my goddamn salvation.

She commands my every move, leading me away from the mess I made and over to the loveseat. We stop in front of it, and she motions for me to sit. I drop down instantly, willing her to tell me what to do. I'll do anything for her. Everything. She only has to ask.

Tasha moves to sit next to me, but I can't bear the thought of her being that far away from me right now. My hands shake as I grip her hips and guide her to sit on my lap so she's straddling me. I know it's a bold move, I know it's too much, but Jesus, I'm trembling, every nerve exposed and raw, calling out to her, my Tasha, to make it better. To make *me* better.

"Oh," she gasps, though she instantly settles into my embrace. I bury my face into the side of her neck as I wrap my arms around her waist, holding her close. "I'm right here," she murmurs, her soft-spoken words the only thing holding me together right now.

I'm a fucking wreck, and the last person in the world I want to see me like this is currently clinging to me, keeping all the broken parts of me together by her presence alone.

"Could...would you want…never mind," she stutters out, her voice trailing off.

"Tell me," I demand, then wince at the desperate edge to my voice. "You can tell me anything," I try again.

"I could walk you through a breathing exercise. If you want," she whispers, surprising the hell out of me. "I just...I sometimes get worked up, too, you know? The world gets to be too much. The lights are too bright and the sounds are overwhelming, even if I'm sitting alone in my apartment. It's hard to breathe when I get like that, so I have a few breathing exercises I do. My social worker taught me them. I could show you."

I hate that she's experienced even a fraction of what I do, and I really hate that she needed a social worker. I'll have to ask her about that later. At the same time, however, my heart stumbles all over itself to get to hers. She understands me in a way I didn't think possible. In a way I didn't know I needed.

"Yeah," I rasp. "Teach me, little one. Teach me anything. I'm yours."

A shiver runs down her spine and I trail my hand over her back, pressing her further into me. I crave every damn thing about her and need her closer, need to consume her, need to carry her light around with me.

"Empty your lungs all the way," she murmurs, her lips barely grazing the shell of my ear.

Fuck, I exhale forcefully, one hand on the small of her back while the other slides up her bare thigh, gripping her flesh. God*damn*, what is she doing to me? I want to cry in her arms and fuck her savagely at the same time.

"Good," she breathes out, tickling my sensitive flesh with that one word. "Now inhale for a count of four." I do as she says, relishing the feel of her breasts pressing against my chest as we breathe in together. "Hold for a count of four, then exhale slowly, for another count of four."

Tasha curls her fingers around the back of my neck, stroking the back of my scalp as she coaxes me to relax and breathe with her. I'm completely consumed by the goddess in my arms. She controls the breath in my lungs, every beat of my heart. It's all for her.

Slowly, slowly, each count of four at a time, my muscles uncoil and the tight knot in my stomach loosens. Oxygen floods my system as my breaths grow deeper, relaxing me even more.

"Better?" Tasha whispers, her mouth only a few inches from mine. Her fingers comb through my hair and I close my eyes, leaning back into her touch.

"You make everything better," I tell her honestly, the words falling from my lips before I can think better of it.

When I blink my eyes open, I see her bright green irises studying me, picking me apart, digging down into the depths of who I am, and seeing if there's anything worth saving. She sways closer, closer, her breath tickling my skin and making me aware of every single place we're touching.

Tasha licks her lips and I follow the movement with my eyes, silently begging her to lick *me* instead.

And then she fists my hair, pulling it tight against my scalp. I groan in pleasure and shock, jerking my hips up and rubbing my hard-as-fuck dick against her hot little pussy. Tasha looks surprised at her bold move, but before she can doubt herself, I seal my mouth over hers and get my first taste.

My little goddess moans so softly, so sweetly for me as I press my lips further into hers. Tilting my neck so I can taste more of her, I play and experiment with her soft little mouth while I trail my fingers up her torso, under her thin shirt, feeling her supple skin quiver at my touch. I cup her breast, brushing my thumb across her pebbled nipple, swallowing down her whimper.

Her hips roll forward and I feel her hands grazing down my stomach, cupping the bulge in my pants. She presses her chest against mine, causing me to growl deeply.

Fuck, she's exquisite, her pliant lips parting beneath my kiss as I lick into her mouth and stroke my tongue against hers. Tasha clenches her thighs together, squeezing my hips between her legs and urging me to take more, taste more, play more.

I'm about to rip Tasha's nightgown right off her body and suck on her mouthwatering tits, but a loud knock on the door startles us both. Who the hell could that be?

CHAPTER 7

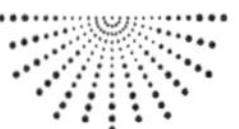

TASHA

"Oh my God," I gasp breathlessly. I'm not sure whether I'm saying it because the knock on my door scared me or because my whole world just got turned inside out with that one kiss.

"Expecting company?" Austin grunts, leaning in to kiss the side of my neck.

"N-no," I whimper, hardly recognizing my voice. I can't help it. The man is touching me and feeling me and teasing me with his lips and tongue as they dance across my sensitive skin.

The knocking starts again, and I tear myself away from Austin, who growls like I just took his favorite toy away. The thought of being this big, burly mountain man's plaything shouldn't send a wave of liquid heat coursing through me, but God, it does. My pussy throbs even as my mind races to catch up with what just happened.

I kissed Austin. Or he kissed me. I'm not sure who started it, only that we both fell into a trance once our lips met. I finally got the answer to my question on how you breathe when you're kissing. Turns out when it's as incredible as what I just shared with Austin, air doesn't matter. The most important thing is more, more, *more.*

But what about Flynn? The voice in the back of my head reminds me.

Yeah, Austin isn't the only one my body seems to respond to. Never have I had this reaction to a man, and here I am, ready to throw myself at not one, but two of them. What is happening to me?

"I know you guys are in there. I see your car in the parking lot, Austin."

"Oh my God," I say again, my eyes going wide. I feel like we were caught red-handed doing something we weren't supposed to. Even stranger is that I feel like I'm being unfaithful to Flynn. I don't like that feeling at all.

"Of course it's Flynn," Austin mutters, taking a deep breath. He's not panicking like I am. In fact, he seems more annoyed than anything else.

"Coming," Austin growls.

"I bet you are," comes Flynn's voice from the other side of the door. Oh my God, does he know what we were doing? Is he pissed?

Before I can spiral too much, Austin stands up abruptly, keeping me locked in his arms. "Wh-where are you going?" I murmur, tightening my hold on him as he strides through my small apartment.

I hear the lock clicking open on my door and I turn, looking over my shoulder in shock as he opens it with me still wrapped around him. I'm sure I look every bit the disheveled mess I feel like after Austin's kiss destroyed me.

Quickly, I scramble out of his arms, embarrassment covering me in a thin sheen of sweat. I can't look at Flynn right now. If I saw betrayal in his bright blue eyes, I might burst into tears. My emotions are all over the place and above all else, I don't want to hurt either of these men. I want them both in my life somehow, even though I know it's a silly fantasy.

I'm about to hide behind Austin when Flynn reaches out, circling his fingers around my wrist and gently tugging me so I'm facing him. My eyes find his like they're drawn by a magnet. Instead of anger or hurt, I see heat and hunger.

"I-I..." I gape up at him, at a complete loss for words.

Flynn's gaze turns dark as he takes a step closer, crowding me against Austin's chest. Austin wraps an arm around my waist, keeping me pressed against him as Flynn tucks a few strands of my wild hair behind my ear and cups my face.

He dips his head down, brushing the shell of my ear with his lips. Flynn's warm breath tickles my skin, making me moan softly.

"Did Austin kiss you, beautiful?" he whispers, sending another shiver down my spine. Austin slips his hand beneath my shirt, stroking up my thighs and stomach with his calloused fingers. It somehow both comforts me and sets me on edge, making me want something. Something...*more*.

"Yes," I whisper, unable to lie to this man in front of me.

He makes some tortured sound in the back of his throat as he trails his lips down my neck, nibbling my skin and kissing away the sting.

"Did you like it?" he rasps.

My breath catches in my throat at his question, simultaneously turned on and scared to tell him just how much I enjoyed having his best friend ravish me. "Yes," I admit, my voice barely audible.

Austin groans from behind me, dipping his head to kiss the other side of my neck.

"Would you like me to kiss you, too, Tasha?"

I nod frantically and Austin nips at my neck, pulling the skin between his teeth and sucking. Flynn gives me a sly smirk, his blue eyes turning dark and gleaming with desire as he leans in closer, closer, closer...

His mouth crashes down on mine, shattering every doubt I've ever had. I'm caught up in the way he eagerly explores my mouth, tasting me and treasuring me, and turning me on even more. I'm barely aware of being moved, the three of us shuffling inside my apartment, tangled up together.

The door closes with a bang, though I hardly register the sound. Flynn pulls me into his arms, groaning as sips from me in hungry strokes. His fingers tangle in my hair and angle my head to the side so he can deepen our kiss. I'm lost in the way his tongue caresses mine, the minty taste of his kiss, the way his breathing is shallow like mine. The kiss lasts for so long I think I might pass out from lack of oxygen.

Suddenly, Flynn rips his mouth away from mine and turns me around, giving me a light push into Austin's arms. I barely have time to suck in fresh air before Austin kisses me as well. His lips are soft, his kiss surprisingly gentle and so unlike the way he devoured me earlier. He takes his time to explore me, giving me long, languid strokes of his tongue that make me roll my body against his.

Once again, I'm spun around, fast enough that I stumble a bit. Austin's hands grip my hips to steady me, pulling me back so my ass is brushing up against his very obvious erection. Flynn smirks, cupping my cheek in one massive hand while brushing a few strands of my hair away with the other.

"Do you have any idea how stunning you are?" Flynn whispers into my lips before kissing me again, softly this time. Austin plants kisses up and down my neck, making me melt against him, even as I grip Flynn's shirt to pull him closer.

God, having both of their warm, chiseled bodies pressed against mine, surrounding me with their strength, their touch…it's perfect. Absolutely perfect. I can't believe they want me like this, but the way they are touching me, caressing me, kissing me, and worshipping my curves, leaves no room for doubt.

Flynn's hands roam down my body, cupping my breasts and kneading them gently. I instinctively bow my back, thrusting my breasts further into his hands.

"Does that feel good, beautiful? You like when I play with your amazing tits?" Flynn murmurs, kissing down the other side of my neck while Austin slides his hands from my hips to the hem of my baggy sleep shirt.

"God, yes, everything…" I gasp when I feel Austin's fingers skim up the inside of my thighs, up and down, lightly touching me, teasing me, driving me wild. "Everything feels so good," I finish, my voice a breathy whisper.

Austin's hand rubs the thin fabric of my panties, making my breath hitch. "Mmm," Austin growls behind me. "Fuck, little one, this pussy is begging for attention, isn't it?"

I whimper and jerk my hips into his touch, practically humping his hand. I don't even care anymore, I'm so lost in this, in them, in us.

Austin continues to slide his fingers up and down my panty-covered slit, just that small touch setting me on edge. When his hand is joined by Flynn's, I can't hold back the moan. Austin pushes my panties aside while Flynn slips his finger into my soaking wet slit. We all groan at what is happening between us.

"Goddamn," Flynn rasps out, circling my clit with his fingers. I squeeze my eyes shut and throw my head back so I'm resting on Austin's shoulder.

Austin turns his head and nuzzles into me, his sweet

gesture making me want all sorts of dangerous things, like to keep these two forever. "Tell us if this is too much," he whispers, his hands trailing up from my thighs to where the waistline of my panties is, teasing me slightly by dipping his fingers inside.

I instinctively suck in my gut, but Austin spreads his hand over my belly and pulls me closer to him, nipping at the shell of my ear. "This thick, juicy body is perfect for us. Don't hide, not from us."

My breath hitches at his words and I swallow down tears. Those words hit me deep. I've spent so long blending in, not drawing attention to myself, content to slip by in life unnoticed. But right now, I feel like I'm the center of their universe, like I'm as essential to their survival as they're quickly becoming for mine.

I'm so wrapped up in what is happening, I almost miss the fact that Flynn rips my panties right off me. I squeal, but he captures the sound with a punishing kiss.

"Hey!" I whisper-shout once we break apart. "I liked those panties!"

Flynn just grins and kisses me again while Austin slides one finger in and out of my tight channel. I gasp at the invasion, twitching in their arms. "I bet you'll like this more," Flynn whispers, replacing Austin's hand with his own.

He's right. I like their touch, their attention, their *everything* more than I like my panties. More than I like anything, really, and that should scare me. However, I don't have time to be scared when I have two mouths kissing my neck, my face, my chest, anywhere they can. I don't have time for doubts when four hands are touching me, massaging me, and bringing me more pleasure than I've ever known.

I've lost track of who is touching me where. All I know is that I'm being stretched and stroked by two gorgeous men who can't seem to get enough of me.

"Oh God," I gasp when I feel a finger circling my asshole.

"Anyone ever touch you here, little one?" Austin asks, his voice tight with need.

I shake my head no and press back into him, making him groan. I hardly recognize this wanton woman I've become, but I can't say I don't like it. Flynn and Austin give me such confidence, how could I not give myself over to this unquenchable lust?

"Fucking hell, sweetheart, you're going to be the death of us," Flynn whispers before kissing me again.

Suddenly, there's one finger in my ass and one in my pussy, thrusting in and out, filling me fuller than I've ever been before. "Wh-what? Oh! Ohmygod, Ohmy*god,* please don't stop..."

We're all sharing short, ragged breaths as the loud, wet, smacking noises fill the air around us. My nerves sizzle and pop, my legs tremble, and I feel like I'm going to pass out from the overwhelming sensations taking over my body. I wrap an arm around Flynn's neck and then reach behind me and wrap my other arm around Austin, needing both of them to hold me up, to anchor me at this moment.

"That's it, Tasha, shit, I feel it, I feel you," Austin grunts, nipping my ear and shoving two fingers up my ass.

"So tight, so fucking wet, this pussy loves having two men giving it attention, isn't that right, beautiful?"

I whimper and nod, gasping for air and clenching down on both of their fingers as they enter me again and again.

Flynn rests his forehead on mine, and I'm shocked to feel him trembling too. "Let go, beautiful," he whispers. "Let go of every-fucking-thing and come for us."

"I...I..."

"We've got you. Trust us," Austin says, his deep voice like liquid comfort as he fingerfucks my ass.

The moment is so filthy, so tender, so vulnerable, I have no other choice but to surrender to them completely.

My muscles tense and lock up, my breath catches in my throat, and the intense knot of pressure low in my belly begins to throb outward until it consumes my entire being. I'm suspended in the air for a flash of a second, and then the world comes crashing down around me as I writhe and spasm around their fingers.

Flynn swallows my scream as he continues rubbing circles around my clit. Austin moves his hands to my breasts, squeezing them roughly and dry fucking me from behind, rubbing his obscenely hard cock against my ass as I buck against him.

"That's so fucking it," Austin grunts.

I gasp for air and deflate completely, the last of my orgasm dripping out of me and leaving me boneless. The last thing I see before letting my heavy eyelids close is Flynn licking my release off his long fingers.

I'm surrounded by my two strong men, each holding me up, pressing light kisses on my head, my face, my shoulders, wherever they can reach. Four hands soothe me, gently bringing me back down. They are treating me like I'm precious, like I just did them a favor instead of the other way around.

"You okay, sweetheart?" Flynn asks, tilting my head up and staring into my eyes.

"Y-yeah," I nod.

"Was that too much?" Austin asks, cupping my cheek and turning my head so we're eye to eye.

"It was perfect," I sigh. Austin grins at me, which lights me up from the inside out. I think I'd do just about anything to put a smile on his usually somber face.

The next thing I know, I'm being lifted in the air and cradled against Flynn's chest as he steps further inside my apartment. God, we hardly made it in the front door before they pounced on me and brought me unimaginable pleasure.

"Whoa, what happened here?" Flynn asks, surveying the spilled coffee, broken table, shattered vase, and scattered flowers.

I felt so awful when Austin spilled the coffee, and then again when he got flustered and knocked over the flowers. I saw him shut down and curl into himself, burrowing down into the anger, shame, and roaring lies in his head. I had to help. I had no idea what I was doing, but sitting with him, *on* him, and working through that breathing exercise was so natural.

"An accident," I say casually, looking up at Flynn's face as he raises an eyebrow, waiting for more of an explanation.

Austin grunts and scrubs a hand down his face before adjusting the intimidating bulge inside in jeans. "What are you even doing here?" he asks, not bothering to acknowledge Flynn's question. "Thought you were working."

Flynn plops down on the loveseat, adjusting me so my legs are draped over his lap. I feel the evidence of Flynn's arousal as it presses against my ass. I can't help but wiggle a little bit, pulling a painful-sounding groan from Flynn's lips. I grin up at him and then curl into his chest, burying my face into the side of his neck and inhaling his sandalwood scent. He combs his fingers through my hair, gently massaging the back of my neck.

I let out a relaxed breath, every muscle in my body turning to liquid as I sink further into Flynn's embrace.

"Stan just got back from paternity leave and was looking for extra shifts. I figured I'd much rather be here with you guys," he shrugs, trailing his hand from my neck down my back, stroking me gently.

Austin nods and grunts as he starts to clean up the mess scattered around my apartment. I smile at his gruff tone, knowing he's nothing but a big teddy bear on the inside. At least for me. These two are so different, and yet perfect for me. Flynn is attentive, patient, and kind. What you see is what you get. His charm and confidence put me at ease like he could handle anything life throws at him.

Austin has been shaped by his pain, whatever it is. That broken part of him calls out to me, and all I want to do is cover his weaknesses and protect his fragile heart. He may be intimidating in size, and rough around the edges, but he belongs to me as much as Flynn does. We fit, all three of us. What the hell does that even mean?

Flynn places the sweetest kiss on my forehead, nudging me up to look at him.

"Are you sure you're okay? That was...intense, and I'm sure a little unexpected," Flynn asks.

I feel my cheeks and neck burning bright red, but I swallow back my embarrassment, trying to hang on to the confidence I felt just a few moments ago when I had two amazing men pleasuring me.

"It was intense," I agree, choosing my words carefully.

Austin surprises me by kneeling down in front of me, taking my hands in his. He looks up, those deep, dark brown eyes peering down into my very soul.

"But I loved it," I whisper, fighting the urge to bury my face into Flynn's chest to avoid eye contact with anyone. I can't believe I admitted that to these men, and yet at the same time, it makes sense. They both make me feel safe and comfortable to say whatever is on my mind. More than that, they seem to hang on my every word.

"I loved it, too, beautiful," Flynn murmurs, kissing my temple and cheek.

"Me, too," Austin growls, leaning forward to nip at my bottom lip and then kiss me sweetly before pulling back.

"Now what?" I ask after a few moments of silence. Flynn

is still rubbing my back while Austin is crouched on the floor, tracing patterns up and down the inside of my arm, pausing every once in a while to circle the extra-sensitive pulse point on my wrist. The way these two are soothing me and treating me like I'm precious has me fighting back tears.

"Now you tell us everything about yourself," Flynn says easily, as if it's the only obvious answer.

"There's not much to tell," I shrug, looking down at my lap. I don't want them to know how pathetic I am, how isolated and anxiety ridden. Then again, they've already seen me at my worst, and they're still here, caressing me, soothing me, and making me feel so loved.

"I don't believe that for a second, sweetheart," Flynn murmurs, nuzzling into the top of my head and breathing me in. "Love the way you smell," he says so softly I hardly hear him.

"Love the way you taste," Austin says roughly before kissing the inside of my wrist.

It's clear these two gorgeous mountain men firefighters want me. Not just my body, but my past. My present. Hopefully, my future as well.

I take a deep breath and start at the beginning. "Well…I never knew my parents," I whisper.

"Relax, precious," Flynn says softly, rubbing the back of my neck. "You're so tense you're shaking. You can tell us anything. Everything."

In typical Austin form, he grunts his agreement, then scoots closer so he's sitting on the floor right next to me. His hand engulfs mine, grounding me and calming the raging storm inside. I didn't realize how hard it would be to open up to them.

"I know," I sigh, releasing some of the tightness in my muscles as I surrender once again to their care. "I just don't talk about myself much. Or ever, really. In foster care, I learned to keep my head down and play by the rules. Every new home I was placed in had different rules and I got confused and in trouble, though I didn't know why. So I just tried to blend in, you know? Keep quiet, don't ask for much, stay out of the way."

"Oh, Tasha," Flynn whispers, wrapping his arms around me and rocking me back and forth. It may seem silly for him to hold me like this and cradle me like a baby, but I've never had anyone treat me this way, never had anyone hold me through my tears. I'll take whatever kindness he's giving me. "I'm so sorry you grew up like that. Austin and I need your light, sweetheart. Don't hide it from us."

I nod my head as the first tear falls.

"Promise us," Austin demands, his intense dark eyes pleading with me. "Promise you'll always be honest with us, with what you need."

"I promise," I whisper, never breaking eye contact. Flynn kisses the side of my temple while Austin nuzzles into the palm of my hand. How the heck did this happen? How are two muscled Greek gods tending to my every need, both physically and emotionally?

"Would you come spend a few days with us?" Flynn asks softly like he doesn't want to scare me away.

My heart leaps into my throat at his words. I haven't spent a single night away from my apartment since I moved in here months ago. The thought of brushing my teeth in a strange bathroom and sleeping in an unfamiliar bed sends my pulse racing. My temples throb with the first signs of a headache.

I hate that I'm like this. Would I like to spend the night with my two sexy, sweet, protective firefighters? Hells yes. But once again, I'm imprisoned by my fear of the unknown, my thoughts racing with all the possible ways it could go wrong.

"Hey," Austin says quietly, weaving his fingers in mine and squeezing lightly. "No pressure. We just want to spend time with you."

"Yeah," Flynn agrees. "We want to get to know you more and explore what's going on here. We'll go at your pace, beautiful. You're in control here, always."

I rub my lips together, darting my eyes from Flynn's kind blue gaze to Austin's dark, almost severe brown irises.

"Do you trust us, little one?" Austin whispers, his eyes locking onto mine, refusing to let me go.

"Yes," I answer without hesitation. I do. I didn't realize how much until this moment.

"Then let us take care of you," he insists, his thumb circling the inside of my wrist once more.

"B-but what about…" I sigh and look around my little living room, not sure how to put what I'm thinking into words. *What about my neurotic routines and my familiar bed and the schedule I stick to every evening and every morning? What about my slight OCD tendencies and extreme social anxiety? What happens when they realize I'm not just shy, I'm practically paralyzed when faced with the unknown?*

"We'll do whatever makes you comfortable," Flynn jumps in, derailing my crazy thoughts. "We already know how you spend your evenings, so show us how you spend your mornings and the rest of your day."

"Are you sure?"

"Never been more confident about anything in my life, beautiful," he says with a warm smile.

"Please?" Austin asks, his voice ragged with a pleading edge to it.

I close my eyes and take a deep breath before jumping off the deep end.

"Yes," I breathe out. "Yes, I want to stay with you."

"Thank fuck," Flynn rasps, nuzzling into the side of my

neck. Austin, of course, grunts, making me smile and squeeze his hand as Flynn presses a soft, sweet kiss to my temple. "There's nothing to be afraid of," he whispers. "We've got you."

I nod my head, willing myself to believe him. The crazy thing is, I think I just might.

CHAPTER 8

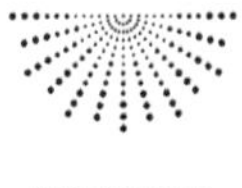

FLYNN

I wake up rock hard and aching, my cock throbbing at the memory of my very detailed, very filthy dream. Wrapping my hand around the insistent fucker, I stroke myself slowly, flexing my hips as I fuck my hand.

Jesus, when Austin opened the door with Tasha wrapped around him, I lost my mind. They were both flushed and breathing heavily. I had very clearly interrupted a moment between them, but as soon as I saw Tasha's swollen lips and glassy eyes, all I could think about was tasting her sweetness.

I was worried we pushed her too far, but our girl was insatiable, eager to have more of our touch.

I jack myself off with rough tugs, unable to stop. Memory after sweet, torturous memory of yesterday floods my mind; her tight little pussy clenching around my fingers, her sticky, warm wetness coating my hand, her breathy moans of pleasure. And her taste...holy fuck, I can't wait to lick up her juices straight from the source, hopefully soon.

Groaning, I pump my fist up and down my swollen length, erupting all over myself like a fucking teenager. That's what she does to me.

I lay on my back, sweating and panting from my intense orgasm. Looking over at the clock on my bedside table, I see it's only a few minutes past seven-thirty in the morning. Perfect. I can have breakfast ready by the time the two sleepyheads get up.

As much as I wanted all three of us in the same bed, I knew it would be too much for our sweet, shy girl. Plus, Austin and I only have queen-sized beds in our rooms, so fitting all three of us would have been a bit of an issue. So, just like that first night in her apartment, I suggested she stay with Austin.

It was already a big day for our girl, both physically and emotionally. Holding her on my lap, stroking her hair, and rubbing her back was unexpectedly intimate in a way I've never experienced before. I know Austin felt it, too, when he kneeled down in front of her and pleaded with her to stay with us for a few days.

I felt the moment she surrendered. Tasha's muscles tensed and she took a fortifying breath before letting it all go and giving into our care. We'll make sure she never regrets it.

Rolling out of bed, I shuffle into the bathroom and clean myself off in a quick, cold shower. I throw a pair of sweats and a T-shirt on before heading to the kitchen.

I check the fridge and pantry to see what I have to work with. I'm a pretty decent cook, thanks to my mom. She always told me a man who can cook will get the girl in the end. I'm praying to every god I can think of that she's right. I don't know what I'd do without Tasha in my life. Even though Austin and I have known her less than a week, she's ours.

"Hey," comes the softest, sleepiest little voice. I spin around, smiling at my adorable woman as she rubs sleep from her eyes.

"Morning, beautiful," I murmur, closing the distance

between us and wrapping my arms around her. It pleases me to no end that she leans into me and gets up on her tiptoes to press her lips to mine.

I groan into her kiss, slipping my tongue inside her mouth and tangling it with hers. Tasha rubs herself against me and I growl, nudging her legs apart with my knee. She instinctively grinds down on my leg, seeking relief for her dripping pussy. Christ, I can feel her wet heat soaking the thin cotton of my pants.

"Starting without me?" Austin rasps, suddenly standing behind Tasha. I was so lost in the way her lips molded to mine, I didn't even notice him walking into the kitchen.

He brushes his lips down her neck, nipping at the sensitive spot beneath her ear. Tasha whimpers and fists my shirt, pulling me closer as Austin sucks on her skin and slides his hands underneath her shirt.

Our sweet girl is so turned on she's trembling, each exhale coming out as a breathy whimper. I can't fucking take it anymore. I need a taste of her arousal, need to bury my tongue in her pulsing entrance and drink her down.

Austin must be just as desperate for more of our girl. He spins her around and lifts her up, carrying her through the kitchen into the living room, sitting down with her straddling him. I follow close behind, sitting next to them on the couch, taking it all in.

Austin squeezes her ass, grinding her down on his lap. She breaks the kiss, turning to me while he kisses down the side of her neck.

Tasha reaches out, grabbing my shirt and pulling me closer. We kiss once more, deeper this time. Austin lifts her off his lap, effectively breaking our kiss. I growl, which makes Tasha giggle. He stands up and pulls her up with him, getting her sleep shorts off in two seconds flat. She goes for the waistband of his sweatpants, tugging them down as I watch with rapt attention, palming my own cock.

Austin pulls off his shirt and is standing there in just his boxer briefs. Tasha turns to me and motions for me to stand beside her. I jump up so fast I grow light-headed. She works my pants off while I rid myself of my shirt.

Tasha pauses to catch her breath. She stares at us, her green eyes shining with lust as well as uncertainty. I see her anxiety bubbling up and making her doubt us, doubt what's going on.

"Hey," I say softly, using up every bit of strength not to grunt at her to strip down and let me gorge on her pussy like a beast. "You're still in control here, Tasha," I remind her.

"If it's too much, we can slow down," Austin rasps.

"N-no. D-don't stop," she whispers. "I'm just...I'm just..." she shrugs and then wraps her arms around herself as if protecting herself from our reaction. "I'm, well, I'm me and you are both so perfect. I don't want to disappoint you."

My heart is torn in two at her confession. On one hand, I love that she spoke her truth and gave words to her insecurities. It shows how much she trusts us, even when it's hard. I'm so damn proud of her. On the other hand, the lies she believes about herself and her worth are going to be a problem. One Austin and I will be all too happy to take care of. We'll show her how desirable she is, how fucking crazy she makes us just by existing.

"Little one," Austin says, sounding as pained as I feel. "Every single part of you is beautiful. You're ours, just like we belong to you."

"Why do you call me that?" Tasha asks, looking up at him with wide green eyes full of vulnerability. "I'm anything but little," she mutters.

"Tasha," Austin growls before softening his voice. "You are *my* little one. You fit perfectly in my arms. Everything about you is perfect." I had no idea he was capable of such tender words, but then again, she's changing everything about us for the better.

I nod in agreement, kissing her forehead. "Austin's right. There's nothing, not one single thing about you that isn't stunning. Do you trust us, beautiful?"

She looks at me and then turns her head to look at Austin.

"Yes," she says, barely a whisper. To prove her point, she raises her arms above her head, shaky though they may be.

Together, Austin and I lift her shirt over her head. Tasha bites her lip and tries to wrap her arms around herself.

Austin takes her hands in his, pulling them back down to her sides while I trace over her full, round breasts, topped with light pink nipples. Cupping them in my hands, I brush my thumbs over her pebbled peaks, groaning at her soft flesh and diamond-hard nipples.

"You're stunning, sweetheart. All of you. From the top of your head to the tips of your toes, and everything in between," I murmur as I lean down and lick a stripe up her cleavage.

I take one breast in my mouth and suck her nipple until it's impossibly harder, making her moan before she can get her protests out like I know she wants to. Austin kisses the back of her neck and pulls her hips into him, pressing her juicy ass against his hard cock.

Tasha cries out when I pull her sensitive nub through my teeth while pinching the other one in between my fingers. I step back and spin her around so Austin can see every inch of her. I see his eyes drink in her porcelain skin and beautiful body. His large hands stroke every available inch of her delicately. Austin leans down and kisses her so gently.

"Perfect. My perfect little one," he whispers into her lips before kissing her again. He trails kisses down her neck, her collarbone, and then he nips at her breasts, making her whimper.

I suck on the tender spot between her neck and shoulder. Tasha tangles one hand in Austin's unruly hair and reaches behind her to cup the back of my neck, pulling me closer to her.

I spin her toward me, causing her breast to pop out of Austin's mouth, payback for when he tore her lips from mine. Lifting her up, I lay Tasha down on the couch with her head on the armrest.

I settle in between her legs, needing my first taste of her. I'm already addicted to every single thing about her, and I know once I'm inside of her, I'll never want to leave. I lift one leg over my shoulder, and then the other, running my nose up and down her slit, just breathing her in. God, she's already trembling, anticipating what's to come.

I part her lips with my thumbs and flatten my tongue, licking every inch of her pussy I can, ending with a swirl around her little clit. I look up from between her legs and see Austin standing by her head, leaning over to palm her breasts, pinching and tweaking her nipples. She bows her back off the couch, simultaneously thrusting her pussy further into my face while giving Austin better access to her perfect tits.

When I see her reach out for his cock, I almost lose it. But that's nothing compared to when Austin takes himself out and she licks the drop of precum leaking out of the head. Austin pulls her up the couch slightly, until her head is hanging off the armrest. I scoot up so I can still taste her juicy cunt.

"Fuck, are you sure?" he asks, the tortured groan sounding so damn painful I feel it in my gut. "You don't have to do anything you don't want to. This is about you, Tasha."

"But last time was all about me, too." Our girl looks up at

Austin with a sexy little pout, one that makes my cock twitch as I continue to lap at her, keeping her right there with us.

"It'll always be about you," Austin vows, stroking every inch of her he can reach from his position leaning over her.

"And if I want to...to..." Tasha blows out a breath and I finally lean back, gasping for air myself. She whimpers and bucks her hips, her body seeking more pleasure. Our greedy girl will get it. She'll get whatever the fuck she wants. "If I w-want to...suck you off?" she asks, her voice so damn sweet and innocent.

Christ, it makes me a dirty old man, but I love it.

"Goddamn," Austin growls. "You can do whatever the fuck you want with me, sweetheart. I'm at your fucking mercy here."

Tasha licks her lips and opens her mouth, making Austin and I groan.

Slowly he feeds her his dick and she moans around him, causing him to growl. Fuck, that's hot, watching the two of them give in to their pleasure. It spurs me on in my mission to make her come.

I slide my hands under her ass and pull her closer to me once again. Tasha bucks beneath me as she slurps on Austin's cock. She pops off of him to beg me for more, harder, deeper. Tasha whimpers like a good girl for me, like my sweet, sexy queen as I bow before her and pay my dues.

She sucks on Austin once more, and I, in turn, suck her clit. Hard. I suck until she's panting and her fingers dig into my scalp. Her feet thrash, kicking my back. She releases Austin, too focused on what I'm doing to her to do anything else. I suck until she cries out, until she gushes, until she loses all control.

And then I keep going. I devour her until she's past her orgasm, deeper than anywhere she's ever been before. I drink her down, lapping at her clit like a man possessed. Tasha holds her breath, her body tense and wired tight. She unravels beautifully for me, letting out all of the tension in one long sigh.

Then, like a good girl, she opens her mouth for Austin while he thrusts inside of her. I swallow down the last of her release right as Austin growls and roars out his orgasm. Tasha swallows every drop, her pussy convulsing one last time as Austin empties himself into her.

Austin pulls out of her and helps her sit up while I lower her legs from my shoulders. Tasha gets on her hands and knees, crawling over to me. I sit up on my knees as well, which puts her face right in front of my raging cock. Tasha looks up at me and fucking licks her lips.

I pull my dick out and watch as she kisses the tip, making me throw my head back with just that little touch. Then, she licks me up and down, massaging the vein on the underside of my cock until I'm shaking.

"I need inside that pretty mouth of yours, beautiful," I grit out, barely hanging on. Tasha has mercy on me and opens up that hot little mouth of hers, sucking me down till I hit the back of her throat. "Fuck!" I choke out, weaving my hand in her hair to keep her there. It feels too damn good to have her move just yet.

Tasha moans around me, the vibrations ringing throughout every muscle and nerve in my body. I snap my eyes open and see that Austin is kneeling behind her, his fingers pumping in and out of her pussy.

I groan at the sight, and Tasha starts bobbing up and down my shaft, hollowing out her cheeks. I swear I've never felt anything like it.

"Jesus Christ, Tasha. That mouth…" I groan.

Austin does something to her and she bucks her hips, which sends her forward, stuffing more of me inside of her magical mouth.

"That's it, Tasha. Suck on his fucking cock. Shit, you look so hot like this."

Tasha moans and works me over faster, harder, swallowing around me until tears form in her eyes. Austin bends over and kisses her spine while blurring his fingers over her clit and palming one of her tits. I feel my orgasm building, tingling in the base of my spine.

"Fuck, fucking hell, I'm not gonna last much longer," I warn. Tasha opens up impossibly wider for me and swallows me down her throat. I jerk my hips, rutting into her mouth uncontrollably.

My orgasm slams into me, as I shoot my load into her mouth. She swallows, again and again, her throat massaging the head of my cock each time. Finally, I pull out of her as she gasps for breath.

A second later, Tasha moans as her arms give out. Austin straightens up and pulls her body up with him, giving me access to her pouty pink mouth. He keeps fingering her right through her orgasm as I capture her moans with a kiss. She comes again in a shuddering, violent wave of ecstasy. Austin and I hold on to her as she rides it out, both of us kissing and caressing her as she slowly comes down.

We collapse on the couch, all three of us absolutely spent.

"Holy fuck," Austin pants, still catching his breath.

"Yeah," Tasha giggles, lifting her head from where it was resting on the couch so she can kiss Austin on the cheek. He reaches out for her, but she rolls away, right into my arms, a bright smile on her face.

I dip my head down and nuzzle into the crook of her shoulder, breathing in her sweet peach scent, mixed with her sweat and our combined releases. It's my new favorite smell, and I hope our home will be filled with it every day from now on.

"You okay?" I murmur, placing a soft kiss on the side of her neck.

"More than okay," she sighs contentedly. "I didn't know I could feel that good. I wasn't embarrassed at all, I was just...I was just able to let go and feel. I…never mind," she trails off, her bold confidence slipping by the second.

"I love hearing how we make you feel," I reassure her, brushing my lips against her temple. "I want to know every thought in your head, sweetheart. You never have to be embarrassed around us."

Austin nods his head, grunting in agreement. I shoot him a look, letting him know she needs his words right now, not just his growly sounds. He relents, taking a deep breath.

"Little one," he starts, cupping her chin in his big, rough hand and gently turning her to face him. "Every new thing we learn about you makes us love you more."

I'm not sure who's more shocked—me, Austin, or Tasha.

I mean, yes, of course, I love her. I knew Austin was well on his way, but I'm glad to know he's all in now. As for Tasha, our shy yet brave girl...she may need more time.

Austin's face is flushed, his confession clearly taking everything out of him. When Tasha just gapes at him, I step in, not wanting him to feel rejected and shut down.

Wrapping an arm lightly around Tasha's waist, I pull her against me and kiss the top of her head. "Love you, too, sweetheart. Knew it the first moment I held you. I know that's big and scary and a complete unknown for you. For us, too," I tell her truthfully. Austin and I have shared women before, though it was so long ago and nothing, *nothing,* compared to being with Tasha. And we haven't even been inside her.

"You both...love me," she whispers. Tasha looks from Austin to me, her brilliant emerald eyes shining with tears.

My heart drops to the floor, thinking we rushed her into

this intense relationship too fast. But then she surprises me by kissing me, her soft, pliant little mouth moving over mine before she trails kisses down my bare chest, placing one right over my heart.

Tasha turns to face Austin, curling up into his side as she peppers kisses over his chest and neck, brushing her lips against his scars. She's so good to him, to me, too. There's no going back. She's it for us.

"I'm scared," she whispers, her little hand finding mine. I lace our fingers together and bring her hand up to my lips, pressing a kiss there. She smiles at me, but the apprehension is clear in her eyes.

"I know," I tell her. "Do you trust us?" I ask her once again. She's said she trusts us before, but this is different. She's trusting us with her heart.

"More than anyone," Tasha answers, her words like a balm to my soul.

"Then let's navigate this together, okay? One step at a time. You're still in control," I remind her. She relaxes a bit, nodding her head.

"I...I trust you. Both," she whispers, looking up at me through her long lashes and then catching Austin's eye as well.

She was close, so damn close to telling us that she loved us, too. I'll take her trust, though. I'll relish every piece of herself she gives us, and one day, I hope her trust can grow into the kind of deep, dedicated love Austin and I already have for our girl.

"Good," I tell her with a grin, kissing the side of her cheek before hopping off the couch. "I already ate, but I can still make you breakfast if you're hungry," I say while getting dressed.

"You already ate?" she asks with an adorably confused

face. “Oh!” Tasha exclaims, her cheeks burning bright red when she finally gets my double meaning.

“Best damn breakfast ever.”

Austin grunts as he kisses the side of her neck. Tasha giggles, the sound filling our cabin with hope and happiness. Now we just have to convince her to stay forever.

CHAPTER 9

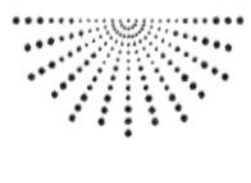

AUSTIN

"Austin! Austin, help me!"

I tear through the trailer, searching through the flames and smoke for the source of my sister's cries for help. She screams just as something explodes in the kitchen, probably the stove.

My heart stops beating.

My world stops spinning.

And then I run toward her with a single-minded focus. Flames lick at my skin, but I barely feel the sting. I toss the debris of our burning trailer out of the way, grunting through the pain as metal slices through my hands and wood scrapes across my knuckles, leaving a thousand splinters embedded deep under my skin. My lungs seize up and I choke on the thick smoke billowing around me.

None of it matters. I have to get to her.

"Celia!" I shout when I see her trapped underneath rubble, flames surrounding her.

It takes too damn long to lift the biggest piece off of her tiny body, and by the time I do, I know in my gut it's too late. I immediately reject that reality and fall to my knees in front of my ten-year-old sister's body. I lift her up and hold her to my chest, sprinting back through the fire to get her outside. Maybe it's not too late.

Fuck, she can't die. She can't leave me.

"Austin," a soft voice filters in through the knot of guilt and pain twisted up in my chest.

I can't open my eyes yet, my mind still holding onto fragments of that day. The trip to the hospital. The doctor telling me she didn't make it. A dozen doctors and nurses restraining me and dragging me into my own hospital room where they cleaned my considerable wounds before shipping me off to surgery.

"Austin, wake up," the voice comes again, this time full of worry and profound sadness. It tugs at my heart and shakes off the last of my nightmare.

I snap my eyes open, breathing heavily as I look into the deep green irises of my little one. Unshed tears well up in her gorgeous eyes. Are they for me? I don't deserve her care or concern. She reaches out to cup my face, but I jerk my head away.

I'm not sure how to process the strange mix of grief and gratitude, abandonment and yet finding my home in those damn green eyes. I'll tarnish her pure heart with my darkness. In no world do I get to keep someone like Tasha forever, but the thought of letting her go makes my heart lurch painfully in my chest.

Clenching my fists at my sides, I swallow down the anger welling up inside me, knowing I'm not good enough for Tasha. I'm not good enough for anyone. My lungs constrict, making my chest grow tight as I inhale shallow, worthless breaths.

Fuck, I feel the beast in me clawing its way out, wanting to lash out and push this sweet, innocent woman away. All the raw emotions churning in my gut make me snarl and grit my teeth, like the monster I truly am.

Tasha surprises me by gently climbing on top of me and wrapping her arms around my neck as her thighs squeeze my hips. She rests her forehead on mine, her deep breaths tickling my lips and taking the edge off ever so much.

"Breathe with me," she whispers. I shake my head no, every muscle in my body trembling, every nerve ending raw and throbbing with pain and lust. What the hell is she doing to me? "Breathe in for a count of four," she presses on, not letting me push her away.

I'm powerless with her soft body clinging to my much harder one. I have no choice but to surrender to whatever spell Tasha has cast over me.

Slowly, we breathe in and out together, and just like that first day, the panic, rage, and fear slip away. With each inhale, I soak up my little one's comfort, her kindness, her endless goodness. With each exhale, I let go of the nightmare, the darkness, and every goddamn thing that would threaten to tear us apart.

"I couldn't save her," I rasp, the words torn from the very depths of my darkness. Tasha doesn't say anything, she just rests her head on my shoulder and strokes the back of my head in a calming gesture, just like she did yesterday. "It was always just my sister and me growing up," I whisper, surprised that I'm telling her about this, yet powerless to stop now that I've started. "My mother was around, but she was drunk or high most of the time. I was all my younger sister, Celia, had. And I failed her."

Tasha cups my cheek, turning me to face her. She places the sweetest, most tender kiss on my forehead, as if to clear all the bad memories away. I wrap my arms around her, holding this goddess of pure light and goodness against me, hoping to soak up more of her magic.

"It's not your fault," she murmurs.

"It is," I grit out, clenching my jaw. "I was supposed to

protect her. I knew my mom started smoking and drinking heavily again, but I left for my job anyway. I was the only one bringing in cash, but it was an under-the-table job since I was only fourteen at the time. I shouldn't have left her alone with our mother. I should have dropped her off at the library or taken her with me to the job site. I should have—"

"It wasn't your fault," she repeats. How can she think that?

"I knew better," I insist. "Mom fell asleep on the couch, cigarette in hand. Our trailer was a pile of shit that went up in flames almost immediately. The fucking bitch woke up and ran out of the trailer without even looking for her daughter. I mean, how the fuck..." I growl deep in my chest at the painful memories bubbling up.

"Austin..." Tasha trails off, tears clogging her throat.

"I showed up after my shift to see flames licking the windows of the trailer and my mom sitting on the front lawn, crying as she watched it all go up in smoke. I knew Celia was inside. I couldn't see her at first, only hear her cries for help. By the time I got to her..."

I can't say anymore. I can't think about it or I might fucking cry in Tasha's arms.

"It wasn't your fault," she says again, clinging to me as she kisses my temple and says it over and over. "It wasn't your fault."

Her lips find mine, or maybe mine find hers. She cups my face in her small hands and kisses me, slow and deep. Her fingers slide to the back of my head as she pulls me in, her kiss growing needy, desperate, almost.

This is what I need. She's my absolution, my salvation. After breaking my heart open for her, I need to feel her like this, need this closeness.

My hands slide up her bare thighs, kneading her soft flesh and making her whimper into my mouth. I swallow down her sexy little noises, tasting them on her tongue as she begins to rock her hips on top of me. Fucking hell, her hot, wet little pussy is grinding against my painfully hard length.

"Tasha," I murmur once I break the kiss.

The moonlight bounces off her brilliant emerald eyes, showing me more of her vulnerability and strength. She doesn't say anything, she simply presses her lips to mine, leading us in a tender kiss.

"Everything okay? I thought I heard yelling," Flynn says from the doorway to my room, his voice scratchy from sleep. "Oh, shit," he growls once he gets a good look at our girl straddling me.

Tasha looks over her shoulder at Flynn. I can't see her face, but Flynn lets out a soft, low growl as he stalks forward and climbs onto the bed.

I slip my hands underneath Tasha's little nightgown, groaning when I realize she's bare underneath the thin fabric. "Naughty girl, walking around without panties on."

"Fuck, are you dripping for us?" Flynn asks, sitting behind her and smoothing his hands over her shoulders, down her back, and underneath the hem of her nightgown. We both take time exploring our girl, feeling her creamy, supple skin beneath our fingers.

I slide my hands around to her juicy ass, gripping her excess flesh and grinding her down on my lap. Flynn groans and kisses the back of Tasha's neck, making her shiver. Christ, I can feel her pussy lips pulse against my raw, sensitive cock.

Our girl moans loudly when Flynn cups her breasts and pinches her nipples. Her hips flex, causing me to tighten my grip on her.

"I...I want..." she trails off, rubbing her lips together in her signature nervous gesture.

I cup the side of her face, rubbing my thumb lightly over

her lips until she relaxes them. “What do you want?” I whisper.

“You can tell us anything,” Flynn adds, kissing up her neck and nibbling on the shell of her ear.

"Oh, God," Tasha moans quietly, leaning back against Flynn. She steadies herself with her hands spread out on my chest, then begins grinding against my lap in earnest, using me as leverage to go harder and faster. "I want...I want you. Both," she rushes to say, every muscle in her body trembling.

“You have us, beautiful,” Flynn whispers.

“But I want you…” Tasha trails off, then takes a deep breath, pushing past her fear and anxiety. “I want you inside of me. I want to feel it, feel you both. I…” She sucks in another lungful of air, her eyes locking onto mine. “I’ve never done this before,” she admits.

“Holy fuck,” I growl, reaching out and cupping the back of her neck. I pull her toward me, our lips crashing together in an explosive kiss. We’re both panting for air by the time we break apart. We’d be the first to claim her? No, fuck that, we’ll be the first, last, and only.

“Are you sure about this?” Flynn asks.

“I’ve never wanted anything more. Never trusted anyone more. Please?”

Flynn and I both groan and help rid our girl of her shirt, revealing her perfect, curvy body, large breasts, and wide hips. Somehow, Flynn got naked, probably when I was too distracted by Tasha’s kiss.

I help Tasha off of me, but we’re only apart for a brief second while I tear my clothes off. Flynn is keeping our girl nice and needy, stroking his large hand over her breasts and down her torso, cupping her dripping wet sex.

Tasha gasps and lets out the sexiest little whimper, sounding almost pained. I scramble onto the bed, needing more of her. All of her.

My little one reaches out for me, combing her fingers through my hair almost reverently. Her touch is tender, but her eyes shine with a dark and desperate need. The combination is my undoing. I still don't deserve this precious girl who chases away my demons, but she's ours now.

I pull Tasha into my arms and turn her on her side so she's facing me. Trailing my fingers up her thighs, I follow the rounded curve of her hip and the slight dip of her waist, up, up, up, until I cup her cheek and draw her closer to me.

"Are you sure?" I murmur before kissing her forehead. My wild lust claws at me from the inside, but I think she needs this reassurance from me right now. I also need her to tell me she's ready for me.

"I'm sure," she says with a quiet conviction that seals her fate to ours.

"Fuck, sweetheart," Flynn groans from the other side of Tasha. He's resting against the headboard, stroking his dick while he looks at us. Tasha turns her head and leans over to kiss Flynn.

When she finally comes up for air, Tasha faces me again, her eyes gleaming with lust and confidence. She bites her bottom lip and grabs the back of my neck, pulling me closer, until our lips are millimeters apart.

"Please?" she whispers before pulling my bottom lip between her teeth and biting down enough to sting. I growl into her mouth and mold our lips together, claiming her, fucking her with my tongue the same way I plan on doing with my huge cock. Mercilessly.

Tasha pulls away from me, gasping for air. I take the opportunity to roll on my back, taking her with me so she's straddling me. Tasha gasps and steadies herself on my chest, smiling at me wickedly.

The little minx starts rubbing her pussy against my cock, dripping her juices all over me and driving me insane.

"Tasha…" I groan, grabbing her hips and sinking my fingers into the soft flesh. I want to lift her up and spear her with my dick, but I still her movements instead. "This is it, little one. There's no going back after this."

"You're ours," Flynn murmurs, leaning over to kiss her temple and the side of her neck.

"I thought I already was," Tasha responds.

"Damn right you are," I growl. I pull her down onto my chest, trapping my dick between our bodies. Tangling my fingers in her hair, I tug on the strands until she's looking at me. "And we want everything with you," I tell her, my voice rough and on edge. I keep one hand gripping her hair, and trail the other one down her back, squeezing her juicy round ass. "*Everything.*" She hums and then presses back against my hand. I dip a finger into her slit, dragging up her arousal and circling her tight, puckered asshole, applying slight pressure.

"Yessss…" Tasha hisses.

I grunt in approval, pushing the tip of my finger inside. "I'm going to take this ass. I'll ride you rough and dirty, fill you up, stretch you out so I can slide in there any time I want. And you'll love it. You'll beg me for it, my sweet, dirty girl."

Tasha moans and kisses me with such fierceness I swear to Christ I could come from that alone.

"I want it," she pants. "I want everything," she says in between her wild kisses. I slide my finger in deeper, pumping in and out of her. She writhes on top of me, her body trembling with the need for release.

Fuck, her tight little asshole pulses around my fingers. I can just imagine the way she's going to feel when it's my cock instead. Mustering up all the strength I have left, I withdraw my fingers.

"Not today, Tasha. I need to stretch you out first. I also need inside of that pussy before I lose my goddamn mind."

"Yes, please," she moans. Her eagerness is going to be the death of me. I don't think I'll ever be able to turn her down when she's offering herself up to me so freely, so full of desire. She's not trying to shy away from it, which is hot as fuck.

I'm barely aware of Flynn moving around on the bed until he's positioned behind her, running his hands up and down her sides.

I release Tasha's hair from my grip and push her up, lifting her hips so she's hovering over me. Tasha smiles down at me, her green eyes sparkling with excitement and nerves.

Flynn whispers something in her ear, then licks a stripe up her neck, swirling his tongue over her pulse point. Tasha moans and nestles her soaking wet pussy right on the tip of my dick. She wiggles her hips a little bit to get herself lined up, pulling a strangled noise from the depths of my being. She's already too fucking good at this.

I almost lose my shit when she stares down at me, her nostrils flaring, her pupils blown wide, her big, round tits bouncing with every labored breath she takes.

"Go slow," I grit out.

"You're in control," Flynn reminds her.

Tasha nods, then locks her eyes onto mine, never looking away as she slides down my cock. My hips jerk involuntarily, the sensation of her pussy squeezing me nearly unbearable. Jesus, she already feels fucking amazing and I'm barely halfway inside her.

"Ohmygod, so deep, so, so deep..." she chants as she grinds down on me.

Flynn kisses the side of her neck while cupping her breasts, pushing them together. The sight is enough to make me thrust my hips upward again, the head of my cock tapping her innocence.

Tasha whimpers, then drops down, taking all of me and letting me fill up her snug little pussy all the way.

I'm about to grip her hips and hold her still so she can get used to my size, but she shocks the hell out of me when she lifts up and engulfs me in her heat once more, swiveling her hips to find what feels good.

A fierce sense of pride rushes through me, knowing we have our girl so crazy with lust she can let go and feel free to explore her own pleasure. "I can't believe I'm gonna..." Her pussy contracts and creams all over me as Tasha digs her nails into my chest.

"Shit, are you coming right now?" I growl. Tasha nods her head frantically as Flynn dips his fingers into her little slit, rubbing her clit in furious circles as she rocks against me.

"Yes, yes, yes…" she whimpers out in broken cries right before she screams out her climax.

"Goddamn!" I roar as my balls draw up tight and I explode inside of her. Fuck, fuck, *fuck*, I wanted this to last longer.

Flynn groans and bites down on Tasha's neck, sucking on her delicate skin before crawling to the other side of the bed. He gets out of the way just in time for me to flip Tasha over on her back and pound into her, filling her up with my cum until it leaks out of her. My dick is still rock hard, so I keep hammering into her, keep snapping my hips, keep fucking her through her orgasm as she whimpers and gasps for air.

Her sounds make my bones vibrate. I grunt as her nails dig into my shoulders and score my flesh, my cock hitting home in one hard thrust after another. The scorching hot sensation of her tight muscles around me makes me gasp into her mouth. Her lips fall open in a silent scream as she takes me in and stretches around me. I rest my sweaty forehead on hers, gritting my teeth against yet another orgasm threatening to overtake me.

"Austin, you feel so good, so, so, good, please..." she whimpers.

"Please, what, little love?"

"M-more...I need...I need...I'm close already..."

"I've got you, dirty girl," I growl, sitting back on my heels so I can grab her wrists and pin them above her head. Tasha squeezes her thighs around my waist as her liquid heat coats my cock, letting me know she likes it.

I glide my free hand up her luscious body cup her breast, teasing her hard little bud before pinching it roughly.

Her pussy clamps down on me almost painfully as she tenses and moans. I ghost my nose and lips up and down the shell of her ear, her shallow breaths and desperate whimpers a beautiful soundtrack I can't get enough of.

"Is this what you need, Tasha?" I growl, kneading her breast roughly as I suck my mark onto her skin. She nods and squirms beneath me as I slide my cock through her folds slowly, so slowly.

"F-fuck me harder," she chokes out, completely lost in her pleasure. I love seeing her uninhibited, free to ask for what she needs. I need it, too.

I pull back and slam my cock into her over and over, the sloppy wet sounds filling the room, joining her cries of ecstasy.

"Oh fuck," Flynn groans from where he's propped up next to her. His voice cracks with his pent-up, painful arousal. "Fucking hell."

Tasha darts her eyes over to Flynn, staring right at him, grunting and moaning as I tear into her savagely.

"Christ, sweetheart," he growls, fisting his cock and grunting right along with her.

Our girl is an animal. She's insatiable, exquisite, dirty, and yet, so fucking pure.

"Need to come now, Tasha," I rasp, my body shuddering

as my orgasm crawls down my spine, making it tingle deliciously. "Come with me," I snarl into the side of her neck, licking up her sweat and nipping her soft skin.

Tasha freezes, her muscles tight, her breathing non-existent as her eyes roll into the back of her head.

Then she shatters in my arms.

I let go of her wrists, placing a fist next to her head and gripping her hip with my other hand. I hold her still while I piston in and out of her, making her tits bounce obscenely with each rough thrust.

Tasha reaches out and grabs Flynn's cock, jacking him off even as she's in the throes of her own climax. Flynn curses as he starts to let go and come all over her chest. He slides his hand in between us once again, circling her clit. Tasha keeps coming, keeps crying out, keeps convulsing.

I hold myself still inside of her and unleash a torrent of cum so forcefully I think I might pass out. My arms give out and I collapse, rolling onto my side. Tasha shudders as I pull out of her, then gasps as Flynn gathers her up in his arms.

"So fucking beautiful," he whispers, tucking her into his side and kissing her forehead.

I manage to crawl up behind her, though it takes the very last of my strength to do so. Christ, I'm still shaking from my life-altering release as I curl around Tasha, resting a hand on her hip.

Flynn combs his fingers through her silky strawberry blonde hair, pushing it behind her ear so he can place sweet kisses up her neck. I'm thankful he's here, taking care of our girl like she deserves. I don't know how to be sweet, but for Tasha, I think I can learn.

"Wow," Tasha whispers. A laugh lodges loose from somewhere deep in my chest. It's been so damn long since I've had a reason to show any emotion at all. Tasha is changing that. She's changing everything.

"Yeah," I agree, nuzzling into the back of her neck. She smells like sweet peaches and sex. Christ, I swear I could take her again, right here, right fucking now. But she needs rest.

The three of us don't say anything for a little while, content to relax and breathe in each other's presence. Tasha breaks the silence, her words slightly slurred as she starts to doze off.

"Wha-at 'bout you, Flynn?" she mumbles, adjusting so her head is resting on his shoulder. She smiles sleepily up at him while he looks down at her with pure adoration in his eyes.

"We have time for everything, beautiful," he whispers, kissing the top of her head. "Just close your eyes for a bit."

Tasha nods and sighs, snuggling up closer to Flynn. We don't really fit in this bed, but there's no way in hell any of us is moving. This is perfect. It's everything I never dared to hope for.

CHAPTER 10

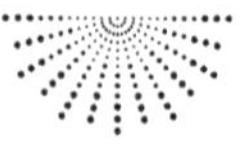

TASHA

I blink awake, feeling more rested than I ever have. I try rolling over but run into a thick bicep that I instinctively know belongs to Austin. I'm still disoriented, so I try turning the other way, only to come face to face with Flynn's chiseled chest.

The rest of my body thrums back to life, each muscle throbbing and deliciously sore. Liquid heat pools between my thighs just thinking about everything we did last night. I don't regret a single second, only that I didn't get a chance to feel Flynn come deep inside me the way Austin did.

I squeeze my thighs together just picturing his muscles rippling on top of me as he fills me up over and over.

As if reading my thoughts, Flynn stirs next to me, his hand reaching out for me before his eyes are even open. I smile, grabbing his hand and guiding it so he's cupping my face. I love the way these two handle me, with such care and respect. I feel utterly adored in their presence.

"Morning, beautiful," Flynn whispers, his blue eyes barely peeking out from under heavy lids. He's so freaking cute and sleepy I can't help but lean forward and kiss him. Flynn slides his hand from my cheek to the back of my neck, winding his fingers in my hair and pulling me closer. "Need something from me?" he groans, rubbing his hard shaft against my hip, letting me feel how much he wants me.

"Y-yes," I stutter out, hardly able to catch my breath long enough to answer.

"What do you need?"

"Everything."

"Fuck yes," Flynn growls, nipping at my bottom lip before licking inside my mouth. I gasp into his kiss as he rolls us over, positioning me so I'm straddling him.

I'm shaking and panting for breath as I stare down at Flynn, my sweet, charming, and attentive firefighter. Right now, he doesn't look sweet or charming. He looks feral. Vicious, even. But I'm not afraid of him. I know neither of my men would harm a hair on my head.

The dark glint in his normally bright blue eyes makes my clit throb. My pussy clenches up and a whimper falls from my lips as more of my arousal spills out of me.

"You're dripping for me, sweetheart," he grits out, gliding his hands up and down my thighs, squeezing my flesh and rocking me against his thickness.

I should probably be embarrassed about that, but I can't find it in me to feel ashamed about anything when I'm with my men like this.

I look over my shoulder at Austin, who is still laying on his back next to us, but his eyes are trained right on mine. His gaze is nearly black, shining with lust. Austin looks up and down my body, studying everything about me. I always thought I'd be self-conscious about being naked in front of another person, but right here, with Austin and Flynn? I've never been more confident.

Flynn circles my hips with his hands, lifting me up slightly. "Never needed anyone the way I need you, Tasha," he growls. Those blue eyes of his soften ever so much, letting me see my caring Flynn underneath the animal he's become. The animal I made him. "Never ached with every part of my mind, body, and soul for another person. I want you more than you could possibly understand, but I need to hear you say it one more time. Are you ready for what this means?"

I fall into the depths of his ocean eyes, drowning in his longing for me. For this. For what's happening between the three of us.

"I need it, too," I murmur, dipping my head down to kiss the side of his neck. Flynn groans softly, the underlying fire threatening to consume us both. "I need you. Please make me yours."

I don't give him the chance to doubt me. Lining myself up with his intimidating length, I slide down his cock, taking him into my pussy. Flynn inhales sharply, his jaw dropping and then snapping shut as he groans like he's in pain.

"Shit, so tight," he rasps, exhaling roughly. "Feels so fucking good."

My inner muscles clench around him, each pulse edging me closer, closer, closer to pure bliss. I want him to feel it. I want to feel it with him.

Flynn grabs my hips, helping me find my rhythm. I hold onto his broad shoulders and use every single muscle in my body to fuck his big dick, riding him as hard as I can.

"Jesus…" he groans, leaning forward and sucking on my nipple. I moan and arch my back, changing the angle so he rubs against my clit with every thrust.

"That's it, little one, ride that fucking cock," Austin grunts, his heavy breaths matching my own. "Does it feel good, Tasha? You like having him stretch you out while I watch?"

"Yes…God, yes," I say on a shaky breath. My legs start to tremble, my whole body tense as I lift myself up and impale myself on Flynn's dick again and again.

I hear Austin moving around, and then I feel his body heat behind me. Austin leans down and kisses my neck, sucking on my sensitive skin and biting me gently. I cry out and grind my pussy down harder, faster, seeking the release my body so desperately needs. Flynn grunts and grabs my hips in a bruising grip, stilling my movements so he can fuck up into me.

Austin cups my breasts and twists my nipples, kissing down my neck and rubbing his hard cock against my ass to get the friction he needs.

"Oh-ohmygod, yes," I stutter out.

My body locks up tightly, my breath catches in my throat, and my head tips back as I grunt and moan out my pleasure. Austin trails a hand down my stomach and circles my clit with two fingers.

"Come for us. Come so fucking hard," Austin murmurs into the shell of my ear before licking me there and trailing open-mouthed kisses up and down my neck.

I'm strung so tight, each of my men catering to my every need, fucking me, sucking me, stretching me, possessing me completely. Flynn slams into me as Austin pinches my clit and bites my shoulder. I'm trapped on the sharp edge of ecstasy, more, more, more, again, again, overwhelming pleasure bites into me, cutting through my core, and splitting me wide open.

I scream as I fly over the edge, free falling into my orgasm. My pussy snaps around Flynn's cock and a flood of wetness spills out of me like a dam bursting. I can't stop. My whole body spasms as I dig my nails into Flynn's shoulders, needing to ground myself in some way. Austin wraps his arms around my torso, holding me tight and not letting go while I ride out the endless waves of bliss.

Flynn roars and then takes my lips in a punishing kiss. I feel him swell up inside of me and then his hot seed spills into my pussy as he rocks my body on top of his, finishing on a groan.

I rest my forehead on Flynn's, both of us panting and shaking. "Fucking incredible," he whispers, kissing me again, softly this time.

I barely have time to nod my head in agreement before I'm being pulled off Flynn's lap and tossed onto the mattress, landing on my back. Austin crawls on top of me, spreading my legs wide open so he can settle his dick on top of my wet slit. He slides his thickness through my folds, tapping the head of his cock on my clit and making my whole body twitch with each thrust.

"So damn sexy, Tasha. Can't get enough of you. Fuck, can you take me again?"

Flynn reaches out and sweeps a few strands of my hair away from my sweaty forehead before resting his there. "Tell us what you want, sweetheart," he murmurs. "We can stop if you're—"

"No!" I whine, hardly recognizing my own voice. The thought of not having my men surrounding me, exploring me, touching me in any and every way, is nearly painful. "Don't stop. Never stop."

Flynn brushes his nose up and down mine before kissing me deeply, almost reverently.

"Never," Austin vows, his gravelly voice vibrating all the way through me. He pulls back and rams his thick cock into my channel, hitting home in one hard thrust. I scream into Flynn's mouth, my entire body spasming as I take more of Austin's length.

Flynn breaks our kiss, gasping for breath. I'm flushed, sweaty, and panting, but Austin isn't done with me. He scrapes his teeth down my neck, my collarbone, and over the tops of my breasts. I arch my back, taking him deeper as he pounds into me. He shows no mercy, fucking me so damn rough as he licks up my sweat and litters my skin with love bites. I want his mark, crave it with every cell in my body.

The sting of his teeth sets me on edge already, and I thrash around underneath him, clawing his back and digging my heels into his ass.

"Fuck yes, little one, that's it, tear me up," Austin growls, picking up speed, fucking me into the mattress. I rake my nails across his skin, needing to mark him, too. He responds by dropping his forehead to mine and grunting with each powerful thrust.

My orgasm slams into me, siphoning the air from my lungs and the strength from my body. Austin pulls out and flips me over on my stomach, grabbing my hips and pulling my ass toward him.

"Again," he barks out, spreading my cheeks open and thrusting into my swollen, sensitive pussy. A jagged moan leaves my throat as I push myself up on shaky arms. I look over my shoulder at Austin, who is staring at where we are connected.

He snaps his head up, staring right at me as he hammers into my little cunt again and again. He looks absolutely feral, grinding and rutting and tearing me up in the best way possible.

I feel a hand on my chin, guiding my face forward. I look up and see Flynn kneeling in front of me, his cock already hard and leaking precum from the tip. My tongue automatically slips out of my mouth and I lick the drop right up, swallowing down his salty essence.

"Do you see what you do to me, Tasha?"

I moan and open up my mouth, letting him slide his rock-hard shaft past my lips. I massage the large, throbbing vein that runs along the bottom, loving the way he grunts with every swipe of my tongue.

Flynn pulls back and threads his fingers in my hair,

holding my head in place. He drags the tip of his dick around my lips, teasing me and making me crave him even more. His cock is wet with my saliva as well as his salty cum. I know my cum is on there as well, the dirty thought making me moan and clench my pussy up tight. Austin grunts behind me and reaches out to play with my tits.

"Gonna fuck this pretty little mouth now. You take what I give you, do you understand?"

I nod my head. Flynn looks up at Austin, who promptly slaps my ass. I gasp, and he does it again, harder. I arch my pack and press back into Austin, wanting him to spank me again. I don't have time to be self-conscious about these twisted urges and desires. The need for my men is too great.

"He asked you a question, Tasha. Answer him," Austin growls.

"Yes, yes, fuck me, I'll take it, I'll take it all," I cry out.

Flynn grunts in satisfaction and tightens his grip on my hair, pulling until it hurts so damn good. I open my mouth wide for him, showing him how much I want it. Flynn slowly slides his cock inside and then backs out just as slow.

Then he snaps his hips and thrusts his cock inside of me, hitting the back of my throat and making my eyes water. I choke on his dick, gagging and crying and loving every second. Austin pounds into me from behind while Flynn fucks my mouth.

I'm completely under their control, two cocks filling me up, using my body for their pleasure. I feel so sexy, so wanted, and despite the hard fuck they are giving me, I feel precious. Austin and Flynn are dominating me in the best way possible, and yet I feel like the powerful one.

Flynn pulls out of me and I gasp for air. He tugs on my hair, tilting my head up so he can kiss me. "So good, sweetheart," he whispers into my parted lips. "So perfect for us, needing two cocks to satisfy you."

His words spark a fire inside of me, one that has been building and building. It flares up and takes over my body when Flynn bites my bottom lip and kisses me again, forcefully this time.

Austin growls and slaps my ass, hammering into me in sloppy, uneven thrusts. I feel him still and then burst inside of me. I surrender to the inferno deep in my belly, letting my orgasm burn through me and swallow me whole.

When I come back down from my high, I feel Austin pull out, leaving me staring at Flynn's angry looking cock. I open my mouth again, taking him deep into my throat. He groans as I suck him down, wanting him to fill me up as well.

I feel Austin's breath on my lower back, and then his lips press down over my spine. He trails soft kisses up my spine and strokes his hands up and down my sides, tracing my curves with his calloused fingers.

The mix of tender caresses and rough thrusts has me tensing up, shaking, overwhelmed, and hypersensitized. Every touch sparks my nerves, pain mixing with pleasure until I look up at Flynn and plead with my eyes for him to come.

He cups my face in his hands and looks at me with equal parts lust and adoration. One last thrust into my throat and I swallow around him, sucking his orgasm from his massive, swollen cock. He holds himself inside of me, shooting rope after rope down my throat while I swallow all of him.

Austin grazes my clit with his finger, and that's all it takes.

I pop off Flynn as my orgasm rips through me. I fall onto the bed and curl up in a ball, tensing, releasing, trembling, whimpering, and wet. So, so wet. Sweat, cum, and tears coat my body.

I'm vaguely aware of being lifted up and repositioned. When I open my eyes, I see Austin looking down at me, his green eyes full of wonder, tinged with concern. I'm curled up in his lap while Flynn sits next to me, rubbing my back in calming circles and nuzzling into my neck.

"Are you alright?" Austin whispers, pressing his lips against my temple.

"Tell us you're okay," Flynn pleads softly, brushing his lips over my shoulder.

I nod my head yes and take a deep breath, trying to clear the fog of bliss making my brain fuzzy. "I...just...I mean...holy shit," I say on a shaky breath.

Austin chuckles, the sound rough but genuine. I feel all warm and giddy inside that I could make the tortured, stoic man happy. "Yeah," he agrees, cradling me against his chest. As impossible as it seems, I feel dainty in his arms, so protected and cherished.

"You're absolutely unbelievable, sweetheart," Flynn sighs, relaxing against the headboard. His hand never leaves me. He strokes my back, plays with my hair, and traces patterns on my bare shoulders while I stay curled up against Austin. "Sexy, sweet, smart, caring...it really is hard to believe you're all ours."

I'm not sure what to say to that. Before I can think any better of it, I stutter out, "Th-thank you." The words tumble out of my mouth, sounding clunky and awkward, but I don't care. It's the first time in my life I've felt so completely safe and loved and like I could do anything without fear. Even be myself.

CHAPTER 11

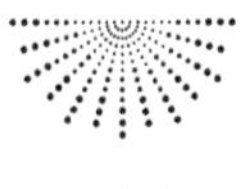

FLYNN

Austin and I dropped Tasha off at her office this morning for her first day back on the job. I hated every second of her getting dressed to leave us. It's a ridiculous, possessive thought to have, but I can't seem to stop when it comes to my beautiful girl.

The only reason Austin and I let her go is because we knew the third floor in her building is sealed off and she'll be working in a temporary office on the first floor. There's no way we'd send her back if there was even a chance she could be in danger.

Still, I feel like I've had a rock crushing my chest since the moment she stepped out of the car. Something keeps nudging me in the back of my brain, something I'm missing, some hidden threat.

Or maybe I'm completely crazy for her. That's another sincere possibility. To say I'm smitten with Tasha is almost offensive. Obsessed is more accurate. I'm in love with everything about her, and I don't care how ridiculous that sounds. Her genuine eyes that sparkle like emeralds when she smiles. Her shy little blush and the way she rubs her lips together when she's unsure of herself. Her sinfully curvy body, sweet kisses, and heated touch. Jesus, the way she moans my name when I'm buried deep inside her tight little...

"Flynn, are you coming?" Austin grunts, throwing me my jacket. I jerk my head around just in time to catch the damn thing before it hits me in the face.

I fucking wish.

"Yeah," I croak, trying to get my wits about me. The chief called about an hour ago and asked if we could come into the station. It's our day off, but when he told us it was about the ongoing investigation with the lumberyard fire, we both readily agreed. We'd do anything to put that horrible incident behind us and get closure for Tasha and the others that the fire affected.

Ten minutes later, we're shaking hands with the chief. He motions for us to sit on the couch in the corner of his office, then calls two cops in.

"Everything okay, chief?" I ask, eyeing the clearance rack Tom Selleck in uniform.

"Just wanted to ask a few questions," Tom, whose real name is Officer Jackson, says. "You boys aren't in trouble, we just have a new lead and want clarification since you were the only ones to go up on the third floor."

Austin nods, leaning forward and resting his elbows on his knees. He definitely went further into the office than I did, so it's really his testimony they're looking for.

The two officers launch into detailed questions about the debris and what Austin saw. I bounce my knee up and down, impatience and frustration coursing through me at the barrage of information they are discussing. I need to get to Tasha. I'm not liking where these questions are leading. Can they not see how our beautiful girl could be in danger?

"Get it together," Austin grunts, elbowing me in the ribs. I jerk my head to look at him, then turn to face the officers.

They are both standing up, and Officer Jackson has his hand out to shake mine.

I must have zoned out a bit, but I'm no less wired and agitated. I shake hands and then immediately excuse myself. There's no way I can stick around for small talk.

"What the hell was that?" Austin growls as soon as he joins me in the hallway. "I think that was the first time I've spoken more words than you have. Like, ever."

I raise an eyebrow at him, hardly able to recognize the man standing next to me. Sure, he looks the same, maybe a little lighter and brighter these days, but still very much Austin. And yet, everything about him has shifted. He's smiling more, and hell, he just made a joke. A lame one, but a valiant effort all the same.

"Tasha," I say over my shoulder as I turn on my heel and jog toward the car we drove.

"What? What about her?" Austin calls after me, breaking into a sprint to catch up.

"I just...fuck, I don't know, I just have this feeling. You won't believe me, and I know it's absurd, but I feel like she's in danger. I know it's crazy, but—"

"Let's go," Austin growls, his voice deep and dark and not to be ignored.

I nod once and start the car, speeding toward Blackthorne Lumber Distribution Center.

A few minutes later, I swerve into the parking lot, slamming the car in park and jumping out of the vehicle. Austin is right on my heels when I swing the front door open and storm inside. It takes me a second to adjust to the dimmer lighting, but when I do, I head toward what appears to be the reception desk.

"How can I—"

"Tasha," I grit out, cutting her off. I try reining in the

crazy and speaking like a human instead of the beast I feel like right now. "Where is she?"

"Oh, uh...you guys are from the fire department?" the receptionist asks. Her eyes shine as she flits her gaze up and down my body. It's not the first time a random woman has checked me out, but I don't like it coming from anyone other than Tasha.

"Tasha," Austin says in a stern voice, stepping up to the desk next to me. He crosses his arms over his chest, putting a lot of his scars on full display. The woman pales and diverts her attention back to me.

"She went out to lunch with her boss, Harry Milford," the woman murmurs in a tentative voice.

"What the hell?" Austin grunts. "She do that often?" He sounds pissed, but I know he's hurt more than anything else.

"It's none of your business," the receptionist snaps, apparently done with answering our questions.

"Let's go," I tell Austin before he says or does something he'll regret later.

We both climb in the car and I start it up, making my way to the nearest restaurant.

"What's your plan?" Austin finally growls, breaking the tension-filled silence. "Drive to every restaurant in town?"

"Yeah," I state simply. "There are only five."

"Could take a while."

"Fine. Do you have a better plan?" When he doesn't respond after a few moments, I nod and continue to Blackthorne Bar & Grille. It's the nicest place in town and close to the distribution center, so I figure it's a good place to start.

"Do you think…" Austin trails off and sighs heavily. "Do you think she's…"

"No," I say sharply, my tone surprising even me. "There's no fucking way she's cheating and you're a dumbass for even entertaining the thought."

I spare a glance at him in the passenger seat, his shoulders sagging as he nods. "I know, I know, I just...fuck." He balls his fists up and pounds one down on his thigh. I'm worried I may need to pull over and talk him down. I can tell he's getting frustrated and worried, and God knows I'm right there with him.

But then something amazing happens.

Austin closes his eyes and takes a deep breath. He holds it for a few seconds and lets it out slowly before starting the process over again. With each cycle of breath, he gains more control of his temper. I have a feeling our brave, brilliant girl taught him that.

Austin hardly waits for me to park the car before he throws open the door and bolts out.

"Wait!" I call after him. "We can't just storm in there, demanding to see Tasha. We'll be thrown out for sure. We have to play it cool."

"Play it...*cool*?" Austin grunts, saying the last word as if it's completely foreign to him.

"Follow my lead."

I manage to get us inside without incident. That is, until Austin sees our girl at a rather intimate table with mood lighting, off in the back corner. He tenses beside me and I can practically hear the roar he's trying to keep contained.

"Can we sit over there?" I ask the hostess, pointing in the direction of Tasha and her boss. I'm hoping to keep Austin in check, just until we get more information. Some part of me knows this asshole is responsible for at least part of what happened with the fire. I talked to him on the phone, letting him know Tasha would be taking the week off with full benefits. He was none too kind to me, but I have a way of getting what I want.

"Let's just grab her and go," Austin grunts.

"We have to strategize," I whisper.

We slip into the booth behind them. Tasha has her back to us, but I can see her reflection in the glass picture frame hanging next to their booth. "I've got eyes on her," I whisper to Austin. "She's okay."

He nods and we place our orders when the waitress comes by. I just read off the first thing I could find on the menu. I don't plan on eating anything. Not until I have my girl back in my arms.

Austin's phone buzzes and I glare at him as he looks down at it and starts furiously typing out a text.

"Is there something more important than this?" I mutter under my breath. Austin finishes his text and turns his phone so I can see it. There's a text from Tasha saying to meet her in the back hallway by the restrooms. We share a look and then try to subtly scramble out of our booth.

Austin paces up and down the hallway while I try to take a few calming breaths as I lean against the wall. I swear we've been waiting for an hour, but that's probably because each second away from Tasha is agony.

Finally, fucking *finally*, she pokes her head around the corner and then rushes toward us. Austin wraps his arms around her in a fierce hug before letting go. I scoop Tasha up and hold her close, kissing her forehead.

"What are you guys doing here?" she whispers once I set her down.

"How did you know we were here?" I ask at the same time.

"I always know when you guys are around," she admits. "It's like I can feel your protection and...and love all around me. That's dumb," she mumbles.

I tip her chin up and brush my lips across hers. "I feel the same, sweetheart. I fucking feel you in my soul whenever you're near."

Austin steps up behind Tasha, gripping her hips and spinning her around. "I feel you everywhere, little one," he whispers, before kissing her sweetly. "Now let's get out of here."

"Wait," Tasha says, surprising us. "I think I can get him to talk."

"What?" Austin asks.

"If...if you guys go back to your table and record our conversation, I think I can get him to confess. He's acting really strange. He never takes me out to lunch."

Austin growls, not liking the idea of anyone besides us feeding our girl. "It's not safe," he replies, his tone final.

"Of course it is," Tasha says with a smile. "You two will be close by. I know you won't let anything happen to me. I need to do this." She's more confident than I've ever heard her, so determined to see this through.

"Are you sure you're comfortable with this, beautiful?" I ask.

"Yes. I'm sure," she doesn't hesitate to answer.

Austin and I share a look. He's apprehensive, but I try to convey my thoughts without putting them into words. She needs this closure, and she wants to be an active part in taking Harry down. Fuck if I'm not proud of our brave girl.

"Fine," Austin grunts. He pulls Tasha into a passionate, claiming kiss, only breaking it when they need to gasp for air. I give her two seconds to recover before doing the same.

She's flushed and a little disheveled, so we help our girl get put back together and send her out to her table. Austin follows her a few moments later and I come out a little bit after him to avoid looking too suspicious.

Sitting in the same spot I was in earlier, I can still see Tasha in the reflection, making sure she's safe. Austin is ready to jump into action if need be, and I'll be close behind. I take out my phone and hit record, barely breathing as we listen in.

"Is there something you wanted to discuss about my work performance?" Tasha asks.

"No, no, I'm just checking in," Harry says, though his voice has a hollow quality to it. "I felt so bad about that fire," he continues. "I mean, what a freak accident, right?" He chuckles, but it sounds forced and fake.

"Yeah," Tasha agrees before taking a shuddering breath. "Well, I'm doing alright. Do you know what caused it?"

"What have you heard?" he retorts. I'm liking this guy less and less by the second, and I already had a low opinion of him before.

"N-nothing," Tasha stutters. Austin growls and clenches his fist. He's done listening in already. He wants to throw punches.

"Where have you been the last few days?" the bastard asks.

"Oh. I was told I had last week off…"

"Yes, yes, but why weren't you at home resting?"

"I was...wait, how do you know I wasn't home?" The realization dawns on me, Austin, and Tasha at the same time. She gasps and whispers, "You were the one outside that first night."

Austin starts to get up but I kick him under the table. "I got this," I mouth to him. He glares at me but settles back down.

"Yes," he hisses. Austin and I hold our breath, waiting for more. "I wanted to make sure you didn't have any serious injuries. I was worried about you."

"Really?" Tasha asks, shock evident in her voice.

"Sure," he says insincerely. "I felt bad about you getting caught up in everything."

"Everything?"

"The fire!" he whisper-shouts. I'm not sure if I caught it on tape, but I'm hoping he says more. "I mean, shit, I didn't mean...fuck," he rambles. Harry's next words come out muffled, like he's rubbing a hand down his face. "Look, I...things got out of hand, I admit that. It wasn't supposed to be that bad. And more importantly, everyone was supposed to be gone." He's becoming more defensive by the moment.

"Wait, are you saying…?"

"Like I said, things got out of hand," he repeats, his voice almost shrill as his words tumble all over each other. It's like now that he's started, he can't stop. "But this is your fault in the first place, really."

"Me?"

"Things were fine before we hired you. It was all going fine. According to plan. And then you go poking your nose where it doesn't belong, bringing up old tax records and unpaid bills. I knew they hadn't been entered into our new system yet, so…" he trails off, letting his sentence hang in the air.

"So you set the building on fire?" Tasha gasps.

"I set one room on fire, and it was supposed to be *contained*. And in case of a miscalculation, the building was supposed to be empty. And then you had to go and get yourself trapped inside."

Austin is shaking, and I know he can't take much more. "I got what we need," I murmur. "I'll call the cops while you go get our girl."

"Already called," he grunts, standing from the table so abruptly it nearly tips over on me. "Time to beat this fucker into the ground."

I stand up with him, turning to face Tasha and a confused, red-faced Harry. Tasha scrambles out of her seat and flings herself into Austin's arms. He wraps himself around her and kisses the top of her head, breathing her in. The entire time, his deadly gaze never leaves Harry.

I lean down and grip him by the collar of his crisp white

button-up. Harry can't be more than five and a half feet tall. He's a wiry little thing, one we'll have no problem teaching a lesson to. Dragging him out of his seat, I look over my shoulder to make sure no one is watching. We're in a dark corner, well hidden from the main crowd of people.

Austin grunts and I look over at him. He nods toward a back door tucked a few feet away. Lifting Tasha up in his arms, he strides to the exit. I follow close behind, tugging along the waste of fucking space middle manager.

As soon as the door to the restaurant closes, I toss Harry down on the ground. His head smacks the pavement and he groans, confused and in pain. "What the fuck?!" he shouts, tripping all over himself to stand up on shaky legs.

Looking into the black eyes of the man who just admitted to starting the fire that could have ended Tasha's life, I feel something in me snap. I cock my fist back and land a hard punch on the side of his jaw.

"That's for putting our girl in danger," I spit out, winding up to go again. This blow cracks his nose, making me smirk with sick satisfaction as he falls back on his ass. I'm about to reign down holy hell on this man, but a soft, delicate hand wraps around my fist, calming me down with just one touch.

I'm panting from the adrenaline and exertion, but I manage to tear my eyes away from Harry long enough to look at Tasha. Her green eyes are shimmering with tears, her brows furrowed in concern. Christ, she's too sweet, worried about me when she just learned her boss almost killed her.

She burrows herself into my chest and I have no choice but to hold her trembling body. I very much want to beat the shit out of Harry, but I know my time's almost up anyway when the police sirens tear through the otherwise quiet streets of Blackthorne.

"My turn, motherfucker," Austin growls.

I gather Tasha up in my arms, cradling her close as I lead us a few feet away, giving Austin space to get the shots in he needs to. There's no way either one of us could let Harry go without a few scars to remind him never to mess with our girl again.

"Are you okay?" I murmur, releasing my hold on her so I can cup her cheeks. I wipe her tears away with my thumbs, then tilt her head up so she has to look at me.

"I'm fine," she whispers, even though I know it's a lie. I wait for her to tell me the truth. I know she wants to, she just needs time to find her voice. "I'm...shaken up, I guess. I didn't know. I didn't know...I didn't know," she repeats, the color draining from her face.

I scoop her up and carry her further away from the scene right as the cops pull into the parking lot. Austin spits on Harry and then wipes his bloody hands on the man's once pristine white shirt before stepping back.

"You're safe now, sweetheart," I whisper into Tasha's hair, placing a sweet kiss there.

"I can't believe you found me," she whimpers, burying her face into the side of my neck. "How did you know?"

"I'll tell you the details later," I promise her. "All you need to know is that we'll always come for you. We'll always protect you." I turn so Tasha doesn't see the police dragging a bruised and bloodied Harry past us. She doesn't need any more violence in her life.

"Thank you." Her voice is soft and broken, but just as sweet and pure as ever. Even after everything she's been through.

"Never thank us for loving you and protecting you. It's our job now." Tasha looks like she's about to say something, her endless green eyes full of emotion and unshed tears. Just then, however, Officer Jackson steps up next to us. Goddamn worst timing.

"Decided to go out and play hero?" he says sternly, his dark eyes never leaving mine.

I shrug and carefully set Tasha down on the ground. I know she'd be embarrassed about having cops see me cradle her like a baby. She wraps her arms around my torso as soon as her feet hit the pavement, and I tuck her into my side, keeping her close.

Officer Jackson grins and pats me on the back. "I'm just messin' with you," he chuckles. "Made my job easier if what Austin said is true. You have his confession on tape?"

"Yeah," I confirm.

"A-and...and you have a witness," Tasha says, surprising the fuck out of me. Her voice is timid, but her courage is shining through. "I mean, I don't know if you need one, but it's me he's talking to in the recording."

"And you're willing to testify against him in a court of law?"

Tasha looks up at me and I give her a soft, reassuring smile. "You know we'll support you either way, beautiful." Her cheeks turn that adorable shade of pink I love so much and she rubs her lips together before taking a calming breath.

"Yes," she says with more determination. "I want—*need*—to do this."

"That will help a lot," Officer Jackson says with a grateful nod. "Will you two come by the station tomorrow to give your statement? We got most of what we need from Austin, but he can come, too, for some follow-up questions."

Tasha and I agree, and the police take their leave, hauling the nightmare of Harry Milford away, hopefully for good.

"I'm so proud of you," I whisper, pressing my lips to her temple, cheek, and on down her neck until I'm nuzzling into her shoulder. "God, you smell good," I mumble, breathing her in.

"My turn," Austin's voice booms from beside me. He's

cleaned up a bit and found a rag to wrap around his knuckles. I reluctantly untangle myself from Tasha and turn her so she's facing him. The two melt against each other as she sobs in his arms.

I spear my fingers through my hair, willing myself to calm down now that the threat is over.

"Let's go home," I say, slipping my hand in Tasha's, and guiding her toward the car. Austin holds her other hand, neither one of us willing to be apart from her for a single second.

"Are you okay?" Austin asks once we're loaded up inside. The two of them are in the backseat while I weave through the streets to get to our cabin in the woods as fast as possible.

"I think I am," comes her surprising response. "I mean, I'm not sure what this all means for my job or what the future holds, but...but I know you'll both protect me, no matter what. I feel like I can do anything as long as I have you guys with me." Her words mean the world to me, and I know Austin feels the same. "Wow, I didn't mean to blurt all that out," she mutters, looking down at her hands. "I'm just emotional, I guess."

I race up the mountain, needing to get her stripped down and in bed so I can hold her.

"Thank you," Austin says, surprising Tasha and me. "Thank you for trusting us with your words, with your needs, and with your safety. You can always talk to us, yeah?"

"Yeah," she murmurs.

The rest of the car ride is silent as we take in the gravity of the day. It's not over yet, but the rest is just details. Our girl is safe and sound, and that's all that matters.

As soon as we get home, Austin and I help Tasha out of the car. He carries her inside, straight to his bedroom. I guess I'm not the only one who needs to hold our girl.

I lock the front door behind me and follow the two most

important people in my life through the house. Austin sets Tasha on the bed and begins slowly removing her clothes. I grab a washcloth from the bathroom across the hall and wet it with warm water.

When I return, Austin is in the middle of taking his shirt off. I kneel down in front of Tasha, gently cleaning off her tear-stained face. I roll the rag up when I'm done and drape it over the back of her neck, holding it there.

"That feels good," she whispers, relaxing even more when I gently massage her neck.

Austin sits beside Tasha in just his boxers, taking over my duties to soothe our girl while I strip down. He helps Tasha get under the blankets, then settles her over his chest, giving me just enough room to crawl in next to her.

We lay there, both Austin and I running our hands up and down Tasha's soft curves, proving to ourselves she's here and she's safe.

"Can I tell you something?" Tasha asks.

"Always," I answer.

"Anything," Austin says at the same time.

"I..." She takes a deep breath and rolls over so she's sandwiched between us, right where she belongs. "I love you," Tasha whispers, looking first at Austin and then at me. Did I hear her right? "Both of you." Those emerald eyes wreck me every damn time. "So much it scares me. It's crazy, right? The three of us?"

"Not crazy," I interject. "Perfect."

"You love me?" Austin whispers.

"So much."

He leans in for a kiss, claiming her and filling her up with everything the man has kept locked inside so long. I can feel it, the bond these two are forming. I'm so fucking happy for all three of us, I might shed a tear or two before the day is over.

"Love you with my whole being, little one," he murmurs, kissing her one last time.

Tasha turns toward me, nibbling on her bottom lip.

"Need to hear you say it again, beautiful."

Her lips curl up into a sugary-sweet smile, tears shimmering in her gorgeous eyes. "I love you, I love you, I love you," she whispers, kissing my cheeks and nose. I capture her lips with mine, licking my way into her mouth and memorizing the way she tastes when she tells me that she loves me.

"Love you more than life itself, sweetheart," I whisper, tucking her into my side. Austin curls up behind Tasha and the three of us drift off, exhausted, yet so very much in love.

CHAPTER 12

AUSTIN

Tasha hasn't been back to her job or her apartment since her boss was arrested a month ago. The trial moved faster than we expected, but then again, arson in a small town tends to make the news.

Our beautiful, brave girl took the stand two weeks ago and answered question after question about the tax documents she found, what she thought had been lost in the fire, and of course, the fire itself.

Tasha was so anxious the night before, she hardly slept. That is, until Flynn and I gave her the release she needed to relax. Even so, we had to run through a few breathing exercises before she was comfortable enough to testify.

I've never been prouder of my little one. She worked through her fear, pushed through the pain, and told her truth. Her gorgeous green eyes found mine and Flynn's over and over, and each time we silently encouraged her to continue.

The three of us have settled into a routine after the excitement of the trial. Flynn and I have tried working our schedule so we get a few days off together and then split our time between Tasha and work so one of us is with her at all times.

Over the last two weeks, Tasha has opened up more and more, getting comfortable with telling us about her past and more importantly, what she wants her future to look like. Our girl likes having a plan, and I know she didn't plan on having two men obsess over her and dote on her every day. She's never once questioned it, though.

Eventually, we got Tasha to confess that she's always wanted to be a math teacher, but she needed a more stable job right out of college, so she went with accounting. Flynn convinced her to look into going back to school.

She hasn't agreed to anything yet, not wanting to accept our money to pay for tuition. We'll wear her down, though. She'll figure out eventually that we'll always take care of her in every way, and spending money on our sweet girl is never a waste. Especially if it helps her achieve her dreams.

"Ready, beautiful?" Flynn calls out to Tasha, who has been busy getting ready in the bathroom for the last twenty minutes.

"Yeah! Yes. Absolutely. Doing great," Tasha says in that overenthusiastic voice that tells me she's on the verge of tears.

Flynn and I jump out of our seats on the couch where we've been waiting for her and rush to the bathroom. Tasha is standing in front of the mirror, taking a few deep breaths. Her strawberry blonde hair is curled into loose ringlets that fall over her shoulders. She has on light makeup, just enough to accent her magical green eyes and plump up her kissable lips.

"You're gorgeous," Flynn murmurs, taking the words right out of my mouth.

Tasha snorts out a self-conscious laugh, then clamps her hand over her mouth in embarrassment.

"What's got you all worked up, little one?" I ask. She starts shaking her head, but then catches herself. I know her instinct is to minimize her problems, but she's starting to trust us with her words, thoughts, and problems.

"I...I'm just...what if they hate me?" she whispers.

"Oh, sweetheart," Flynn says in his most soothing voice. "There's not a chance in hell that's gonna happen."

"Who wouldn't love you?" I add, stepping closer and wrapping an arm around her waist. Flynn stands on her other side and cups the back of her neck gently, massaging her tense muscles and kissing her temple.

Tasha sighs as she melts into us, letting us calm her with our words and tender touches. "It's just a big deal, you know? I'm meeting your mom," she says to Flynn. "And your friends, Clayton and Naomi. I mean, Clayton is a freaking billionaire who lives in a castle! A castle I'm going to visit and dine at!"

Flynn cracks a grin at her and kisses her cheek. "It's not *that* impressive," he says, rolling his eyes playfully. Tasha glares at him but then curls her lips up into the cutest smile.

"Besides," I say, leaning in to nuzzle her neck. "We'll be there the whole time. You know you're safe with us."

"I do," she agrees, resting her head on Flynn's shoulder while I kiss up her neck.

"Come on then, beautiful," he murmurs. "My mom is dying to meet you. She loves you already, I promise."

Tasha nods at first, but then her face goes pale. "Oh my God, your mom!" she exclaims. Flynn and I share a look, both of us confused. "I mean, I knew she was going to be there, I just...how do we explain this." She points at me, then Flynn, then herself. "Us."

"What's to explain?" Flynn asks, completely unfazed by her question.

"We love each other. That's all there is to it," I add.

"But will she freak out? I mean, we're not exactly normal."

"We're better than normal. We're us: Tasha, Austin, and Flynn. And my mom will be happy that I'm happy. And she'll be beside herself when she sees how sweet Austin is."

"Austin is always sweet," Tasha insists. I chuckle and bury my face into her hair, breathing in everything about her. God, she's incredible, and all ours.

"I'm sweet to you, Tasha. You took one look at me and broke me apart. Then you put me back together, piece by piece. Now you're embedded in my soul, little one. Forever."

"Forever," she agrees, looking from me to Flynn.

"Ready to get this show on the road?" he asks, already ushering us out of the bathroom.

"I guess so," she breathes out.

I hold her hand all the way to the car, then climb in the backseat with her as Flynn pulls out and drives up the mountain to Clayton and Naomi's.

We only make it about halfway there when we see a red junker car pulled over to the side of the winding road. The closer we get, I can make out a woman in the driver's seat, banging her head on the steering wheel.

I meet Flynn's gaze in the rearview mirror and nod, letting him know we should stop for her. What kind of firefighters would we be if we didn't help people when we saw their need?

He pulls over and parks right behind her car. I hop out, giving Tasha a quick kiss before shutting the door.

I walk up beside the car and tap on the window, shocking the woman. She looks young and so damn tired. I feel for her. I also have no idea what the hell she's doing out here. The only people who drive up this way are the few loners who live higher up the mountain. It's no place for out-of-towners.

"Everything okay?" I ask. Damn, I should have sent Flynn

out here. The woman looks up at me with wide, terrified eyes, taking in my size and scars.

She shakes her head, then nods, rolling down her window a crack. Her next words are clipped, professional, and a bit cold. "Yes, I'm fine. I'm always fine. I just...I can't seem to get my stupid GPS to work."

I grunt out a laugh, which makes the woman narrow her eyes at me. I hold my hands up in surrender, not wanting to upset her. I look over my shoulder at Flynn, hoping to get his attention so he can come over and deal with this, but he's busy talking to Tasha. I understand, but fuck.

"Doesn't surprise me," I say, trying to sound human. I'm still not good at talking to people who aren't Tasha or Flynn. "You won't get a signal this far up the mountain. I think you're lost, though. There's nothing up here but private property."

"Oh, good! So I'm not totally off course," she says brightly. Her face lights up and she takes a deep breath before gripping the steering wheel, almost as if it's keeping her grounded. "Does Ranger Cason live up this way? The last time my GPS worked, it said to follow this road, but it's so narrow and rocky, I don't even know if it's considered a road."

"In Blackthorne, this is definitely considered a road. One of the nicer ones up the mountain, too." Her eyebrows shoot up her forehead, but she doesn't say anything. "Are you sure you want to see Ranger? He's not exactly thrilled to have guests," I hedge. That's the understatement of the century.

The man has been up on this mountain longer than anyone. Owns a good chunk of land, too, but for some reason, he's still living in a one-room cabin. People make offers left and right to buy up just a portion of his vast property, but he chews them up and spits them out for breakfast, every last one.

"Yes, Ranger Cason. I have business with him," she says in her professional voice. I can tell she's more than a little nervous, but she covers it well, as if she's had a lot of practice.

"Hopefully not to inquire about his land?"

Her head jerks to the side, her eyes finding mine. "And what if I am?" she snaps.

"Look, I'm not stopping you. Just warning you. He's not receptive to offers and he's not going to sell his land. You're not the first to try, and I'm sure you won't be the last."

Her shoulders fall and her head dips down so she's looking at her lap. I notice her grip the steering wheel tightly again before letting go and straightening up. "Well, I don't have much of a choice. Please point me in the right direction."

I do as she asks, giving her more detailed instructions on how to get there. She thanks me in that professional, clipped manner, then pulls back onto the road.

"Everything okay?" Tasha asks.

I nod my head. "Yeah, she was a little lost."

"Where the hell is she going?" Flynn asks, no doubt having the same thoughts I was. This isn't a place for tourists.

"Ranger Cason's," I chuckle.

"No shit?" Flynn starts laughing as he pulls onto the road as well. "I hope she remembers the way back down the mountain. She'll be scrambling to get away from his grumpy ass."

We drive the rest of the way in comfortable silence. I keep my arm around Tasha, stroking her arm up and down to keep her calm. Before long, we're pulling into Clayton's estate. It's freaking obnoxious, but then again, rich people tend to go overboard.

"Whoa," Tasha whispers.

"I know, right? Not that impressive," Flynn says with a grin before unbuckling his seatbelt and hopping out. He pulls open Tasha's door and helps her out, taking her hand in his. I get out and take her other hand, the three of us walking up to the front door together.

We barely get two steps onto the front walkway before the door swings open, revealing Flynn's mom, Angie. She looks at Flynn, then Tasha, then me, her eyes dropping to see all of us holding hands. Flynn is right, Angie is open and accepting and I know she'll be happy for us.

Still, I won't lie and say I'm not a little nervous. Tasha tightens her hold on my hand and I give her a reassuring squeeze.

"Aren't you just gorgeous?" Angie gushes, hurrying down the porch steps.

"Thanks, Ma," Flynn teases. She rolls her eyes at him, then rests her hands on Tasha's shoulders.

"You're perfect," Angie declares. "For both of them," she says with a wink. Tasha blushes and looks from Flynn, to me, before glancing up at Angie. "Love is love," Flynn's mother says, shrugging before giving her son a hug, and then me.

"Are we going to eat or just hug?" Flynn jokes, taking the attention away from me and Tasha.

"You won't be getting any dessert if you give me more of your attitude," Angie says sternly. Her eyes glitter, however, and her lips turn up into a smirk.

We follow her inside where Clayton and Naomi are setting the table.

"Oh my gosh, hey! You must be Tasha," Naomi exclaims, setting down the plates in her grasp so she can throw her arms around Tasha. Our girl stiffens but eventually lets go of our hands to return the hug. "Sorry," Naomi says, backing off. "I'm so excited to have another woman around here to talk to and hang out with."

"Replacing me with a newer model, are you?" Angie calls out from the kitchen. "After all we've been through!"

Naomi giggles and shakes her head. "Never, Angie. Just adding to the inner circle."

"Ah, now that's an idea I can get behind."

Naomi loops her arm in Tasha's and leads her over to the table, chatting away as if they are already old friends. I want that for her. My little one has been through so much and I know she hasn't had many friends in her life. Flynn and I can be there for her and love her as much as humanly possible, but she needs solid friendships, too.

The rest of the night goes by in a blur of delicious food, good conversation, and plenty of laughter from everyone, even me. Clayton balked when we told him about the woman we saw on the side of the road looking for Ranger's place. Angie expressed concern for the poor girl for not knowing what she's walking into.

Eventually, Naomi yawns, making us all aware of how late it's gotten. Clayton kicks us all out and scoops Naomi up in his arms, presumably carrying her to bed. Flynn, Tasha, and I give Angie one last hug before heading back home ourselves. We've got plans for our girl. Big plans.

CHAPTER 13

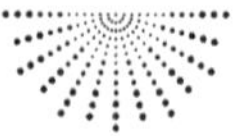

TASHA

That was the most fun I've had...well, maybe ever. I was so anxious about meeting everyone earlier this evening, I almost worked myself up into a panic attack. My men were right there to bring me back from the edge, just like I know they always will.

"What are you thinking about?" Flynn asks, helping me take off my coat as soon as we step inside.

"Just about you two," I answer truthfully. Flynn's eyes grow dark, and I feel Austin step up behind me, his lips brushing against the shell of my ear.

"What about us, little one?" he rasps, his voice deep and dark.

"Well, now I'm thinking all sorts of dirty things," I admit. I'm shocked I said those words out loud, but that's just what Flynn and Austin do to me. They make me feel safe enough to say anything I want.

"You're not the only one," Flynn murmurs before capturing my lips with his.

I open up for him, sucking his tongue into my mouth and taking control of our kiss. I've never been this forward, this bold before, but I don't have time to doubt myself. Not when Austin's hands find the hem of my dress, slipping under the fabric and caressing my inner thighs.

"Fuck," Austin grunts, cupping my pussy and no doubt feeling the way I've soaked my panties. "You want it bad, don't you?"

I nod, breaking the kiss with Flynn. He grunts in frustration, dipping his head down to suck on my neck.

"What do you want, sweetheart?" Flynn mumbles into the crook of my shoulder before kissing and nipping the skin there. "Want us to undress you and worship your sexy little body?"

"Yes," I breathe out, automatically lifting my arms so they can do just that. "Please."

My men waste no time getting me naked, then practically rip their own clothes off. We don't go to the bedroom, all three of us too needy to wait that long. Instead, Flynn guides me a few steps into the living room, standing in front of me and cupping my face.

"Tell us what else you want," he whispers, resting his forehead on mine.

"Y-you," I whisper. "B-both of you." I rub my lips together, gathering my courage to say what I *really* want. "At the same time."

Austin groans from behind me, nipping at my shoulder and licking away the sting. "Goddamn," he groans, sliding his hand down my spine, tickling every nerve ending before he slips two fingers into my slit, circling my tight little asshole.

"Yes, more..." I breathe out, bucking my hips as I seek more friction, more of whatever is going to happen next.

Austin sits down on the couch behind me, skimming his nose down my spine and nipping at the globes of my ass while his fingers grip my hips possessively. Flynn cups my chin, drawing my face toward his so he can kiss me.

Austin rubs his thick fingers up and down my soaking slit, gathering up my juices, and circling my clit. I gasp and fall forward slightly, resting my forehead on Flynn's shoulder while Austin sinks two fingers inside of my pulsing cunt. He groans and removes his fingers, pulling them back towards my ass.

"I'm gonna take you right here, little one," Austin's deep voice rumbles as he pushes his fingers inside my back entrance.

At the same time, Flynn grabs my hair and tilts my head up, searing his lips onto mine, branding me with his flavor. His tongue slides in and out of my mouth in the same steady rhythm of Austin's fingers.

Flynn breaks away from my mouth and blazes a trail of kisses down my neck and over my collarbone until he's sucking on my nipples, back and forth, pinching the pebbled peaks between his teeth and then licking away the sting.

I buck my hips, forcing more of Austin's thick fingers inside of my ass. He grunts and shoves a third finger deep inside, twisting them together until it burns, until my nerves singe with heat, until my skin is coated in fire and my core erupts into flames. My climax claims me, body and soul.

Flynn holds me steady, grunting into the side of my neck, his muscles flexing as I tremble and cry out against him. "You like that, beautiful?" he rasps, licking and biting the tender skin on my neck. "Like coming around his fingers in your ass? You're gonna love when he has his cock up in your tight little hole. Want to feel it?"

"Yes," I whimper, trying to nod my head but not having enough concentration to do anything but surrender.

Austin massages my hips in his large hands and then cups my cheeks, spreading me wide open for him. I feel his breath on my most private place, then his tongue as it circles around my tight ring of muscles. He guides me to sit down on his lap, but he stills my movement when I'm perched right above his cock.

"I'm gonna break your tight little ass in, Tasha. It's ours now, all of you belongs to us, every fucking inch, every drop of pleasure, every tear, every hope, every smile, it's ours."

"Yours, I'm yours, I want it," I whisper, tears stinging my eyes, though not from fear or anxiety. I'm overwhelmed by how much they love me, and from the depths of their souls. I feel so cherished, so used, but only in the best way possible.

I cling to Flynn while Austin positions my legs on the outside of his and then slowly guides my ass down on his massive cock. There's so much pressure, so much tension, so much need vibrating between our bodies I swear I'm about to pass out.

"Breathe, just breathe for me, love," Austin murmurs into the back of my neck. I do as he says and take in air, willing my muscles to relax.

"That's it, beautiful," Flynn encourages, removing my hands from his hips and guiding them up over my head until I'm gripping Austin's hair. "Let him have control. Make him feel good while I make you feel good, okay?"

I nod my head, but I can't really process his words. Austin grabs my thighs and snaps his hips, filling me up and tearing me open while I scream and rip at his hair. Fuck, it hurts, but I'm somehow close to coming already. Austin grunts and holds me in place while he grinds that thick dick deep, so deep inside of me.

"I've got you, Tasha, you're doing so good, so good, fuck me, you feel amazing," he whispers, half pained, half in awe. I'm feeling the exact same way.

I feel Austin spread me open even more as he widens his legs in between mine. Then Flynn's warm breath skates across my chest, his tongue darting out to lick my aching nipples before trailing down my body. I'm aware of every single nerve ending his mouth touches, down, down, down, tongue, teeth, lips, again, lower, again…

Then Flynn sucks my clit into his mouth and shoves two fingers in my pussy and I come harder than I ever have.

Austin roars and fucks up into me, sawing his huge cock in and out of my ass as Flynn eats out my pussy with a ferocious need. One of my hands twists in Austin's hair while the other reaches out and grips Flynn.

I'm completely consumed by them, taken so thoroughly, surrendering my body and heart to every thrust, every lick, every rough touch and tender kiss. I'm about to come again when Flynn stands up suddenly and takes me with him.

I'm spun around and then I'm straddling Flynn's lap as he lays down on the plush rug in front of the fireplace. He sheaths himself inside of me in one hard thrust, entering me completely and stretching my pussy wide open.

I cry out in shock as overwhelming pleasure rushes through me. Rocking my hips back and forth, I grind against Flynn's monster cock, loving the way he shudders underneath me.

"I couldn't wait," he grits out, cupping my breasts and pushing them together so he can lick and nip at my cleavage as he tears my pussy up.

I feel Austin's heat behind me, and then one large hand rests between my shoulder blades as he pushes me forward so I have to brace myself on my forearms on either side of Flynn's head.

"Fuck yes," Austin groans, massaging my ass and helping me grind down on Flynn. "Gonna fill you up all the way. Can you handle two cocks, my sweet, dirty girl? Two big cocks just for you, worshiping you every goddamn day?"

"P-please," I whimper, bowing my back and bucking my hips to show him how much I want him, too.

Flynn cups the back of my neck, demanding a kiss from

me. He pries a moan out of my lips as he kisses and fucks me like we're on fire. Austin grips my hips and eases inside of me. Flynn pulls out and then pushes back in when Austin leaves me. They take turns thrusting into me, hitting places I didn't know I had, bringing me higher and higher, so high I'm afraid I'm going to shatter when I finally come down.

Flynn grunts and slams into me over and over, his movements becoming jerky and uneven. I rest my sweaty forehead on his, needing this connection, too, while my body is being used and ripped apart savagely.

“I’ve got you, Tasha, my beautiful girl. You feel fucking amazing. I love you so much, need you so much, love.”

I whimper and nod my head against his, squeezing my eyes shut and falling into the rhythm of my men filling me and fucking me like we were made for each other.

We grunt and groan together, working as one to reach ultimate bliss. Austin pistons in and out of me while Flynn grinds his massive length deep inside of my pussy, rubbing my clit with the base of his cock and making me spasm and clench around him.

The air is thick with the smell of sex and the obscene, sloppy wet smacking sounds of our bodies coming together over and over, joining as one. My orgasm bubbles up from the very depths of my being, pooling in my belly and trickling out into every cell. My lungs fill with air and I hold my breath as it takes me under, plunging me into darkness, bliss rocking me back and forth in violent waves.

Flynn shouts out a curse and explodes inside of me, triggering another climax to match his own. Seconds later, Austin snarls and snapshis hips against my ass before emptying himself of every last drop. We come together, our combined orgasms spilling out of me and coating all of us until we’re a mess of sweat, cum, tangled limbs, and ragged breaths.

"Holy shit," Flynn whispers once he's caught his breath. He turns his head to look at me, his eyes filled with awe and complete satisfaction. "I mean, just...holy shit," he says again.

Austin lets out a muffled groan of agreement from where he's lying face down on the rug.

I laugh softly, trying to lift my head up. No such luck. I'm too exhausted to move an inch. Flynn scoops me up and lays me across his chest, kissing the top of my head and stroking my back.

"You okay, beautiful?"

"Mmhm," I mumble, snuggling closer to him.

Austin shuffles slightly and turns so he's facing me. His deep green eyes skim over my prone body and then he reaches out to trace my curves.

"I think you broke me," he teases.

I somehow find the strength to grab his hand and kiss his fingers. "How can I fix it?" I whisper while sucking his middle finger into my mouth.

"Tasha..." Austin groans, half in pain, half aroused.

"Holy hell, are you ready to go again?" Flynn asks, still in a daze himself.

I rest my head back down on his chest and lace my fingers with Austin's, keeping him close. "Boys, I don't think I'm going to be able to move from this spot for at least twelve hours."

They both laugh and give me sweet kisses. "That's okay, beautiful. We have forever."

"Forever," Austin agrees.

"Forever," I echo, letting the word sink inside of me and settle into my very core. "I like the sound of that."

"Will you make it official, then?" Austin blurs out. Flynn's eyes go wide and the two of them share a look.

"What do you mean?" I ask, looking from Austin to Flynn.

Austin just smiles at me and hops up, apparently not

exhausted anymore. He walks down the hallway, showing off his sculpted back and muscled ass. I think I could stare at my men all day. In fact, I'd like to do that sooner, rather than later. Something tells me they won't have a problem with it.

I shiver and huddle closer to Flynn, the cold seeping in without Austin pressed against my back. Immediately sensing my need, like always, he reaches out and grabs a blanket from the basket next to the fireplace.

As soon as he has it tucked around us, Austin returns, his hand curled around something. I can't tell what it is, but I suddenly get a crazy, giddy thought. There's no way, though, right?

Austin smiles almost nervously at me before crawling under the blanket and snuggling up next to me.

"Where did you go?" I ask, stifling a yawn. "And what did you mean by 'making it official'?"

"I…we...shit, I should have thought of something to say," he mutters. "It's just, well…"

I hate seeing my big, strong, stoic Austin feel insecure about anything. I reach out and cup his cheek, wanting to comfort him in this small way. He surprises me by lifting his hand up, opening his palm to reveal a diamond ring.

I'm stunned. It's perfect. Too perfect for words. Still, I need to be sure I'm not misinterpreting what he's offering me.

"Wha-t?" The word is barely out of my mouth before Flynn jumps in.

"I think what Austin is trying and failing to say is that we love you like crazy, and we want you with us always, tied to us in every way." I shuffle around so I'm facing Flynn once more. I'm sure my eyes are bugging out of my head, but I nod slowly, hanging on his every word. "We might not be able to have a traditional wedding and marriage, but Tasha, we want it all with you. Be our wife, wear our ring, have our children.

As long as we're together, it doesn't matter what anyone else thinks."

Austin nods his head and grunts, making me smile. I turn and look at him again, my heart melting all over again for my brutally beautiful mountain man. His dark eyes are glistening with tears, and I lean forward, kissing the first one as it falls.

I take the ring from his hand and slip it on my finger, admiring the way it sparkles, and appreciating the weight around my ring finger. It fits perfectly, of course. I know Flynn made sure of that.

"Of course I'll be yours in every way," I whisper, looking up at Austin. "I love you." Leaning forward, I take his lips with mine, hoping to tell him everything without words. He responds immediately, his lips and tongue saying everything I need to know as they work me up, gently, slowly, but with such passion, my chest nearly caves in.

We finally break for air, and Flynn turns me on my side so he can claim my mouth as well. I kiss him back, reaching out for Austin at the same time, winding my fingers around his.

"You're absolute perfection," Flynn whispers into my open mouth. "Our brave, sweet, strong as hell girl."

"You ignited our hearts, beautiful," Austin adds. "And set our souls on fire."

"And now you're ours forever."

"Officially," I say with a wink, grinning at my men as they nod. They said I ignited their hearts, but they're the ones who found mine, dusted it off, and taught me how to love. I can never thank them enough, but I can sure as hell try. Especially now that we have forever.

EPILOGUE

AUSTIN

"Congrats," Clayton says, walking up next to me.

We never talked much before, but these last few months, our women have been hanging out more and more. Flynn, Tasha, and I go over for dinner at least once a week. Clayton and I are still quieter than the others, but we're trying to open up a bit. Naomi is sure working her charm on him, that's for sure. And Tasha? Well, she's gone and turned my whole world upside down.

"Thanks," I cough out, clearing my throat. "And thank you for hosting the wedding. Your property is perfect. I know it's everything Tasha envisioned."

Clayton nods, then searches for Naomi. He doesn't like to have her far from sight. Not that I'm much better with Tasha. Clayton must spot his woman, because he shakes my hand and offers his congratulations again before taking off.

I look for my little one amongst the small crowd of people. The ceremony was short, sweet, and intimate, with Angie giving a few words before the three of us exchanged vows and rings. I'd be lying if I said I didn't tear up a bit.

We're at the reception now, the few people we invited

mingling in the courtyard of Clayton's estate. I know it took a lot for him to open up his home like this for us. I have a feeling Naomi had a lot to do with that.

I never thought my life would end up this way—belonging to a beautiful, compassionate, achingly sweet woman. And sharing her with my closest friend. It's so much more than I deserve.

"Looking for me?" Tasha's airy voice fills me up and I turn to see her walking up to me. I gather her up in my arms and kiss her forehead and nose.

"Always," I tell her truthfully.

"Well…here I am," she whispers, pressing her lips to mine. I tease her with my tongue, then reluctantly pull back, chuckling when she pouts.

"Is today everything you hoped it would be?"

"And so much more," she says with the most genuine smile. I have to taste it. Leaning down, I brush my lips against hers, giving into what we both want.

Suddenly, my woman is being pulled away from me. I growl while Tasha giggles, stumbling into Flynn's embrace. He wraps his hand around the back of her neck and pulls her in for a heated kiss.

"Love you, sweetheart," he murmurs, kissing her again.

I step up behind her, gripping her hips and kissing the back of her neck. "Love you with everything I am," I vow.

"I love you both so much my heart aches sometimes. I didn't think I could love this much, but every day you both prove me wrong." She opens her mouth to say something else, then rubs her lips together, her cheeks turning bright pink.

"What is it?" I ask. "What were you going to say?"

"Well…I wasn't sure how to tell you, and I don't know if this is the right time, but I don't want to keep secrets from you."

My stomach sinks with worry, not knowing what to expect.

"You can tell us anything. You know that, beautiful," Flynn says.

Tasha nods and takes a fortifying breath. "Okay. Well, this morning I found something out. I, um…I'm pregnant," she blurts out, her eyes going wide with her confession.

Flynn cheers and lifts our girl up in his arms, spinning her around and peppering her face with kisses. I'm shocked. Too stunned for words. How does my life keep getting better? I think I'm going to have to grow a bigger heart for all the love I have for Tasha, Flynn, and now our baby.

God, I'm gonna be a dad. I have no idea how to do that. What if I'm terrible? What if—

"I can't wait to meet him or her," Tasha whispers, slipping her hand in mine. "You're going to be an amazing dad. You're so attentive and gentle when you want to be. I know you'll always protect us."

"Damn straight I will, little one," I grunt. Tasha smiles up at me, but it faulters slightly, worry flashing across those green eyes.

"Are you…upset?"

"What? God, no," I rush to say, realizing I haven't given her much of a response. "I'm scared out of my mind, but I'm so damn happy. I know we'll make an incredible family."

"I'm scared, too," Tasha admits. "But between the three of us, our child will have so much love in their life."

"We'll make sure of it," Flynn promises, kissing her temple while resting a hand over her stomach. I place mine there as well, even though I know it's too early to feel much of anything. Still, being close to the little life we created is some powerful, paradigm-shifting shit.

"Thank you," I choke out, nuzzling into the side of Tasha's

neck. "Thank you for giving me more than I ever could have dreamed of."

Flynn nods his head, tucking some of her hair behind her ear. "Both of us," he confirms. "We never could have hoped for a better partner in life. You're it for us, sweetheart. I can't wait to start on our forever."

THE END

Want more Men of Blackthorne Mountain?
Check out Ranger & Chloe's story here!

In case you missed it, click here for Clayton & Naomi's story!

ABOUT THE AUTHOR

Cameron Hart is an Amazon bestselling author of contemporary romance. She writes books with lots of heat, plenty of sweet, and just enough drama to keep things interesting.

Sign up for Cameron Hart's newsletter to get a free novella!

Join Cameron Hart's street team to receive ARCs & help spread the word about new releases.

ALSO BY CAMERON HART

Want more mountain man books? Check out the Bear's Tooth Mountain Men series!

Taming Her Mountain Man

Healing Her Mountain Man

Redeeming Her Mountain Man

Shared by Her Mountain Men

Bear's Tooth: The Complete Series

More books by Cameron Hart:

Moscatelli Crime Family: The Complete Series

Chaos MC: The Complete Series

Claiming His Babygirl

Savage Ride

Curvy Temptations

www.ingramcontent.com/pod-product-compliance
Ingram Content Group UK Ltd.
Pitfield, Milton Keynes, MK11 3LW, UK
UKHW041956190726
13854UKWH00005B/2004

9 798521 370603